The Search for Home

Chris Wu and Janelle Lee

Directed by Claire Qu through the Bookwriting Class.

To Claire, for encouraging me to keep writing this book.

And for Mom and Dad, and my dog.

To Andrew Lee for being the best sibling.

And for Lindsay Zhang for being the best of friends.

Table of Contents

Chapter 1

"Come on, Riley!"

Riley was learning to play fetch. John, Riley's trainer and best friend, was 19 and on his summer break from college. He attended the University of Bryant every fall and spring semester, joined by his girlfriend, Carla.

John and Carla first met when he bumped into her in the hallway. He vaguely remembered how furious Carla had been. Her sea-blue scales had razed John's own midnight silver scales, and the seeds of friendship had been planted. The next day they were partnered together for a group project, forcing them to hang out more often.

After graduating from high school, John decided he couldn't live without Carla. As time went on, the two got closer and closer together. They had walked to the beach and Carla had leaped on John and kissed John in the face. They planned to live happily ever after for the rest of their lives, just like in the fairytales.

John was majoring in science with his girlfriend and best friend, Carson. Carson had a fun, bubbly personality but could be easily angered. John learned that the hard way.

Riley yapped around playfully. Riley was a golden retriever that was two in dog years. She was so annoying. Once she bit him so awfully, he recovered after 12 human years. But John was a different specimen. He and Carla were Jokulan. His friend, Carson, was an Oeamidi. So 12 human years was ½ Jokula years.

"YAPPY YAPP!" screamed Riley. Riley snapped her jaws open and closed. Riley's bites hurt more than the time he burned his hand from cooking pasta with rabbit meat. John had hit Riley with a giant wooden brown spatula by accident. Riley had growled viciously and they had a huge hit and pawing fight.

John yelled "BALI!" which meant idiot in Palinese.

Riley turned around and wacked John with her big, fluffy, white tail. John fumed with anger. Riley barked with frustration. They launched into another huge fight. Suddenly Riley, the stupid golden doodle, raced over and bit John in the right butt cheek.

"Rileyyyy." John cried out in pain and scolded Riley. His bottom felt like it had been stung by a space scorpion. That had once happened before though. John was out in space and attracted a lot of space scorpions.

John went inside to go get a band aid. Ouch. Good thing that the bite wasn't too bad. It could have been much worse. Though, it was somehow on his rear end. This happened very often. Obviously, Riley was being obnoxious.

"Riley, obnoxious dog."

He got some Gator and sat by his girlfriend. He had been dating Carla for nine months, but it seemed as if he had known her for his entire life. She had chestnut brown hair and gorgeous chocolate brown eyes. She worked at the local pet shop, which explained her ability to tame Riley any time. That skill came especially useful when it came to dealing with an overly energetic dog like Riley.

Carla gaped with her mouth wide open in shock. She nodded to John and pointed at his butt.

"Oh, Riley bit me," John said, fighting a laugh.

"Well, I'm sorry to hear that, Johnnyboy," mused Carla, clearly trying not to laugh.

"Carla, is your cousin alright after his Highfli accident? I hope he is." said John, attempting to move the conversation away from the topic of his rear end.

"Oh, of course Johnnyboy. He will be released from the hospital in a couple of days, though I doubt he'll want to see anyone because of the scars on his face," Carla mentioned ruefully.

"I'll pay him a visit sometime. I'm sure he'll want to see me if I bring him his favorite oatmeal raisin cookies," John said.

"Great idea. Let's go bake cookies for him as a get-well gift. You've got all the ingredients, right?"

John nodded and the two headed over to the fridge where Carla quickly snatched up the butter and eggs. Old-fashioned oatmeal raisin cookies were the best.

"Johnny, I am going to make the cookies. You will burn down the place if you get anywhere near these cooking tools," laughed Carla.

"Well, I am going to ride around the planet real quick, Carla, said John. John took a daily eight hour spin around with his Highfli. It was the most peaceful, relaxing, and best time of his day. Though recently, he had been more bored than usual, so his Highfli trips had been getting longer and longer.

"Johnnyboy, stay with me, please," Carla groaned. "I need moral support."

"Sorry, Carla, but I'll pay you back by getting dinner with you tonight."

John pulled up his Highfli. The flashy sports hovercar was as new and shiny as a silver spoon : a blue circle adorned with feathery cushions inside. The controls were easy to use, which was helpful since John didn't bother to read the manuals. He loved it almost as much as Carla did. Okay, he had to admit he liked it more than Carla, washing it every two days.

Carla always complained that John spent too much time cleaning it, but he "only" spent eighteen hours a day washing up the sides, oiling the engine, and cleaning the secret emergency trapdoor. To him, that was time well spent.

Well, look at this baby. John thought.

He made sure Carla wasn't looking because he liked Carla, and she would surely be mad if she saw him kissing his Highfli. John went over back to his girlfriend.

"Here, have some Gator," John said. He had learned from the library that Gator used to be called Gatorade, back when the planet was called Earth. Now, it was called Joluka. He poured some Gator for Carla. Then, he filled the fuel tank all the way to the top with a gas can from his storage boxes and closed the lid.

I love you, he thought towards the Highfli instead of towards Carla.

He flew up to the sky and quickly stopped by his pal Carson. He told Carson hi and then they chatted for a few minutes. Then, they said bye to each other, and *whoosh!* John loved this feeling. The breeze going up his nose, into his small but smart brain. His blissfulness was interrupted by Riley's loud barks. John froze immediately.

"Yap Yap."

"Riley," John snapped, "What are you doing here?" John was mad.

The answer, like usual, was a series of bark. But, it sounded more like shrieking. John was more curious than his Uncle Kirby (who, apparently, was curious about how many times ants brushed their teeth, if ants even did brush their teeth, or if ants even had teeth).

Not only had Riley bit his butt, but she also ruined his plans to travel the world in his lovely cotton laced 100 dollar pants, again. Plus, he hadn't gone on a flight in five hours and a universe tour in 36 hours. John's body ached with the knowing that he HAD to go.

John's silver midnight dragon scale skin was getting hot. John knew this meant that Riley wanted to go with him. Riley always wanted to go with him no matter what which was strange but honestly, reassuring . *Beep!* John activated the oxygen bubble.

This was vital because if he forgot, he would most likely die without the warmth and oxygen. The bubble flowed rainbow and white. He flew past the star Chaos 2397 and Brilliant 62 at the speed of 30 light years per second and saw approximately 3,575,947 black holes. He always counted; it was a wonderful habit.

John thought he saw a sandy clump of dust. He reached to grab it and realized he still had his oxygen bubble. It almost popped. John held his breath and quickly and efficiently, pushed the oxygen bubble.

That was close! John thought. *Silly me.*

It was coming from a place he had never been before and where his dad had disappeared seven years ago when John was only 12 years old. His dad had claimed there was another planet to live on. He had told John stories of white sunsets and long, peaceful nights.

John returned his focus to space and braced himself for impact that might come.

Nothing came. *Huh.*

He watched for a moment the stars he passed by. *Wait, I didn't control the speed!*

"Yappy yap yap" Riley barked annoyingly. John tried to slow down his speed, but he couldn't. The space car was accelerating too fast. And was that a planet in front of him? Uh oh... He really hoped he wouldn't crash land. That would have been awful. But the planet raced towards him, faster and faster.. *BOOM!* Just like that, John crashed, and his vision went white.

He woke up hours later with a jolt.

Wait, this isn't my house. I should be sleeping next to my beautiful Carla!

That was when John realized he had crash landed.

And there was a smell of… poop? Uh oh! John really did not want to pick up Riley's poop. That job was reserved for Carla. John did that once and puked for weeks on end. It was disgusting. Riley's poop was watery and poop brown with a hint of garbage green.

He looked around slowly, realizing he was on planet Dead 974, which was the planet his dad had disappeared on. Most people just called it Dead. He was so dazed from the crash and shock that he quickly fainted.

When he finally came to, he found Riley licking his face. The moment he opened his eyes, sticky, translucent slobber came pouring in. He quickly closed them and wiped all the drool off his scratched face. *Ouch.* But now, how was he ever going to get home? And, what about his promise he had made to Carla earlier? How was he going to sleep with her tonight? John wondered if he would ever see those beautiful brown eyes again. The thought chilled his bones.

But no, wait, there was something more important right now! Where was his Highfli?! John fainted again at the thought of his life savings all destroyed.

The Mighty Highfli! Gone?

John felt like he had been punched in the face. Why did he think coming here was a reasonable idea?

Three hours later, when John was awake (courtesy to Riley's sloppy wet tongue, of course), John took Riley on a walk. Five minutes in, Riley saw what looked like a kakhorro (pronounced ka-KOR-o) shell, and began eating it. John remembered that he'd read about kakhorros, too.

They used to be called cicadas when Joluka used to be called Earth. The second Riley bit into the kakhorro, the kakhorro's giant pincers pinched Riley's poor snout. Apparently, the kakhorro wasn't a shell. This time, it was Riley that passed out.

Once Riley was awake, they continued. Ten minutes later, John got humiliated by a baby monkey.

The monkey, for the start, rustled some leaves that sent goosebumps to John. Riley barked ferociously. The leaves rustled again and Riley barked LOUD, and John's ears were nowhere near alive.

The monkey, which seemingly came out of nowhere, had a shockingly blue coat of fur and a tomato red face. The monkey was way larger than the ones back at home. In fact, the monkey was larger than John and Riley combined. Everytime the monkey jumped, he did a massive curling flip that ended with John and Riley both amazed yet horrified.

The monkey sat there with a proud grin on his face. John wanted to smack the grinning face off the monkey but John knew it was hopeless. He needed Carla, his mighty sidekick. She would've slapped the monkey's face so hard that it would never be able to grin again.

The grin stayed there. John was annoyed.

"Go away, monkey!" The monkey tilted his tomato red face.

Thirty minutes later, Riley was confronted by the same monkey. Riley yapped at the monkey and the monkey busted out the worm dance and scratched his armpits jumping around screaming,

"Oh la la! Oh la la!"

Then the monkey went up to John and picked his nose. His finger came out with a glob berry gooey essence.

"Monkey, gross." John yelled. John ran away from the monkey with Riley yapping nearby. He shuddered at the thought of the monkey.

The monkey was fast, John had to admit that. He ran about three feet before the monkey got him. The monkey wiped his boogers all around John's scales.

"Ugh!" John was angry.

John was so angry that he decided to return the grossness to the monkey. John quickly realized how difficult that task would be. The monkey performed the legendary "humiliation demolition" karate move and humiliated John once again. John was really getting mad now. John cast the epic "return to sender" spell by waving his arms in a pendant way while whispering an ancient language. The monkey had no way to demolish a powerful spell, so he got humiliated.

Once the monkey recovered, it called the kakhorro bug over and waged war on the now furious John. Riley looked like she had a huge balloon on her snout. John quickly readied his amazing rifle and Riley bared her not-so-sharp teeth.

John dodged a spitball from the kakhorro and shot the kakhorro. The kakhorro exploded into a big splotch of greenish-maroon goo. Laying in the center was the bullet tip. The tip was sizzling and smoking.

The monkey used a sword and tried to slice Riley in half. Riley had learned Doggy-Fu and used "Claw Block" and swiped the sword away. The monkey used "Electric Ball" and was rolling toward John and Riley in a rush of fury and destruction. John pulled out his sword on his belt, and poked the monkey. The monkey ran away with electricity particles still on his shabby fur.

Chapter 2

As the monkey rolled away, John found his Highfli all in ruins, burning with such ferocity that John had to shield his eyes. *Oops.* This was bad, his beautiful Highfli was broken. All his hopes of getting back was GONE. BAM. Just like that. John moaned painfully, not just in pain but also in the fear of never going back.

"NO!" John screamed for about two straight minutes, according to his calculations. This gave him plenty of time to conclude why he had such a sucky dog. John HATED sucky dogs. Obviously, Riley was the suckiest of them all. Riley should have totally become queen of sucky dogs. Riley barked ferociously. John's heart still beamed with joy. John felt a pang of sadness as he remembered his loving, caring, and nice father.

Riley clearly didn't care as much as John did though. Riley never met John's dad. She simply barked halfheartedly and chewed on her bone.

Riley came racing over and accidentally came too close, whacking John with the gallon of water he packed.

"Riley," John scolded.

John tripped over a rock, and flew at least 25 yards into the air. Gravity took a little getting used to on this awkward planet. John crashed into a gigantic rock and Riley happily yipped around. Still, gravity was weird. Or so it seemed. John was now scratched everywhere and soaking wet. Now, he didn't have any water. What a nice dog. What a really nice dog. What a really really nice dog.

Once he got up, he saw his dad's car but his dad was nowhere to be seen. John felt a surge of hope; the car had to mean something, right?

John was already searching for a fine sized rock for a funeral. Obviously, he needed it even if his dad wasn't here. The stone was just for his dad's last breath and memory. John searched every corner of the planet in his sight. His dad should be around there because when John was seven, his dad had given him a tracking stone. It glowed blue when John's dad was within 50 meters. It was glowing blue.

John suddenly realized he would probably be underground, since the crash was 43 human years ago. That would be ten Jokula years. John got the emergency shovel from the Highfli crash and started digging. Fast.

John was glowing hot red when he finally found his dad right under John's own Highfli. His dad looked shambled, as if his last breaths had not been pleasant ones. John wept for another three hours.

He remembered a lot of stuff, like how his dad gave him his Highfli that was now broken, how his dad gave him medfruit when he was sick, how his dad had teached him how to walk, how he taught John how to use a gun. The more John thought, the more John cried. He cried until his eyes were dry, and by then, he had formed a small pool of watery, salty tears. *Water.* John thought. Sadly, it was all sandy and salty. When he thought of salt, he remembered the time when his dad accidentally put too much salt in his eggs but John had thought it was delicious.

John kept crying; he cried so hard, he couldn't really breathe. He saw Riley and remembered when his dad came home with a pleasant surprise for her. Riley seemed to know what John was thinking because she started howling too.

Why dad? Why did you die on me? I still needed you. Why? Just why? John thought.

John made a tombstone, and used a piece of metal from the crash to carve a message.

Had John's dad been here all the time? John needed him.

"Dad, why, why, why?"

John would never go to the Jokula Night Club together with his dad. Or see the fireworks on the 7th of Harisai. John was truly horrified and sad. Why had his dad come here anyway? Did he not care for John, Sasha, Mom, Roxanne or Riley? Was he so selfish that he would leave his family? Why had he left? Why had John survived though? John didn't know so he thought about the Heathens. It used to be called Heaven but Heathens sounded better.

John used his tracking senses after about three days of frustration. On this planet the sky was… purple. John suddenly realized that he was struggling to catch his breath. This planet must not have enough nemokek, which was also known as oxygen.

Back at home, the air was clean and cool. It always felt nice and refreshing on his skin. However, on this peculiar planet, the air was musty and humid. It felt absolutely disgusting; it was sticky, warm and strage. John hated the air quality on this gosh-darn planet.

Once he disassembled the car, he found that there was a small fire inside. The fire slowly grew, and John used the flames to wield the steel into many things. First, he made an anvil and hammer, then he made a pickaxe, then a sword. It was crazy slow. His hammer took forever to make. Once he was done, he was ready to go exploring. Then, he remembered the emergency trapdoor. Fortunately, it was untouched.

Inside was his emergency rifle. He found it and went into the hazy unknown.

It was hard lugging the five hundred pound anvil around, so he made a rope from dried tree sap from the tree that he had crashed into. The tree had a gaping hole and sap was oozing out like crazy. John touched the sap. His finger immediately burned bright blue.

Huh, weird. John thought.

Soon, John got so hot that he was forced to drink one-tenth of his meager water supply. The heat burned into his skin, and John would have given anything for more water. He found a small tree and went to the bathroom, thoroughly disgusted by the entire experience.

He ate a sandfruit from the "crash tree" and felt much more comfortable. *Maybe it gives me a cactus effect so that I'm more suited for the desert,* he thought. John started to cry. He knew he was acting like a baby but he couldn't help it. The fruit reminded him of his earliest, happiest memories.

He remembered first learning to walk when he was two years old. He remembered the first time he and Carla kissed. He remembered meeting Carson on the playground when they were six years old. The more John ate, the sadder he got. Suddenly, he spotted a huge cloud coming with deadly shards of dust. No… It couldn't be. John didn't land here with the intention to die. But it was still there, inching closer and closer.

"Sandstorm!" he shouted.

John had to act quick. He grabbed a sharp piece of metal from the crash and decided to call it his "sword". He stuck his hand into the sandstorm. Now, he tried sticking his rear end in. *Ouch, my butt!* Apparently, the sandfruit did not protect against the violent grains of razor-sharp sand. His titanium boots were already scratched and dented from walking on this deathly planet. John was deeply upset. The boots were expensive and hard to find. John made the obvious decision: run.

Shards flew past John and a battery in his pocket, which he had not previously noticed, exploded.

"AHHH!"

There was a big explosion. John's face twisted with pain. His butt was ashen and burnt, but he kept on running. John was mad, and he wasn't normally this angry. John used his sword to block his face from the catching flames.

John fired a bullet into the storm, but the bullet was easily torn into scraps. John hurled a grenade into the "Gateway to The Underworld" and instantly regretted it. The grenade was torn into explosive shards, and then all the shards exploded and the sandstorm bulged just enough to make another battery explode. John's pants had lots of batteries stored in them, which means that it set off a chain reaction. John went flying, and Riley followed. Unfortunately, the sandstorm followed too.

"YIP YAPPY YIP YEE WARRAOOW!"

It was Riley, who limped over to John. It turned out that Riley had been dumb enough to put her paw inside the "whirlwind of death." It came away with streaks of blood. John quickly tore off some cloth from his sweat-soaked shirt with his sword. Now half his shirt was gone so he just took off the whole thing. *Of all the dogs out there, I'm stuck with Twiddle Dee The Wonder Dummy, who is dumber than a turkey.* With Riley's wound all wrapped up, they ran.

Riley barked loudly as a sharp pain went through her paw.

When his underwear caught on fire, John yelled, "RUN FOR YOUR LIVES!"

John thought he heard explosions. He turned around and pinned himself and Riley onto the ground just in time to see a huge fireball being flung from the storm. It singed John's rear end a little for the second time. Ok, John had to admit, a lot.

"Ow," John winced as he patted his pants. He stood up and swung his sword at another fireball. Strangely, the sword didn't melt. The fireball, glowing hot, burning and red, flew straight through the sword. Then, the fireball turned bright green and faded to black and crumbled to ash on John's foot. When John looked at his sword, it was glowing red-hot.

Riley just stared in amazement as John's pants caught on fire again. He shook the pants off, the fire burning and searing hot. Now, they made an odd pair: an injured dog and a naked human being. Well, John did have a white underwear with pink hearts on but nobody needed to know. John felt really embarrassed but nobody was watching him.

I mean, if no one is watching, who cares. Guess I'll be just like this for the rest of my life.

His thoughts were abruptly interrupted by a nearby alien that John had not noticed before.

"Oooohhhh, dude look! It's a Jokula in underwear with pink hearts!" exclaimed the alien.

It snapped some photos not-so-secretly. John heard the noises but didn't fully comprehend what the noises meant. *Wait… was that a camera clicking?* John turned around, but no one was there. The second he turned back around, the clicking began again.

John walked away and continued adventuring, forgetting about the camera clicks. During his treacherous hike, John found some cute little creatures that kinda looked like scorpions. John offered them some bread, ham, cheese, and lettuce. The adorable little critters gobbled the food up hastily. However, the critters quickly became angry at John, as he had no more food to offer. They began to chirp in annoyance, which escalated to biting and scratching. John defended himself with his weapon.

The critters exploded into blobs of poisonous liquid, purple smoke, and neon-green acid. When the strange mixture cleared, four more scorpions stood in John's path. John threw a grenade and instantly killed them.

In the distance, John saw a nice cave.

"Hey, Riley, let's rest there for a while."

They started walking toward the dark, damp, cool cave. He stepped on something, but didn't bother to see what it was. He felt scuttling, but didn't bother to see what it was, either. A moment later, John regretted his actions. As it turns out, he had stepped on a scout, which had split itself into four pieces. John's titanium boots protected him from the poison gas and the acid. The scouts quickly ran into the cave.

John yelled at them and threw another grenade. The scouts were quickly dispatched.

"Should we attack the intruder now?" a deep, rumbly voice said.

"Not yet, I think we should do a proper duel. Aim for some more traditional methods." a higher-pitched voice said.

"Prepare for battle! Everyone in their formations! Get those stingers all juiced up!" the high-pitched voice screamed.

"Uh oh…" John said, terrified, "SCORPIONS!"

Chapter 3

The clattering came closer… and closer… and closer. Soon John could see bands… no, *tribes* of scorpions scuttling out of a cave. Each one was the size of a big tomato with their menacing tails swing back and forth. John shivered. What would happen if one of the tails bit him? Would John ever see light again. John started feeling woozy and scared at the thought of never returning back to John's beloved planet. Finally the last scorpions came out.

There were two scorpions in the center. One had a jeweled crown and another had a bone crown. The woman scorpion was huge, regal, and looked like she could kill John in a single sting from her glittering gold tail. Jewelry was probably her favorite thing in the world. A gold tail band hung on her tail and a black decorated veil covered her face which John guessed hid a nasty scowl. She held her head high like she preferred to be somewhere else and then she swished her tail. Her tail band shimmered like a thousand precious jewels.

The male scorpion on the other hand was also into jewels. He had a natural green band along the side of his body and he was 2x bigger than the regal female scorpion. The male had a gold mask that shimmered like the sun but John knew there was a nasty grin under the mask. He stood up still and held his head low as if he couldn't wait for John to be dead.

He had a shimmering blue cape around his body so it looked like he was very strong or in a strong position.The female and male scorpion stepped forward slowly like they were covered in syrup. They flicked their tail simultaneously. The scorpions started to crawl forward one by one. . . Each had their tail waving around ready to pierce John. They raised their tails, ready to attack.

The scorpions kept crawling forward.

"He-hey, u-um w-we c-could e-explain t-th-this r-r-right? W-we a-a-are f-friends r-r-right?" John asked nervously.

"No." The queen said. Her voice was surprisingly beautiful, like snow, but under it hid something else, something nasty. She waved her tail and John's eye's were immediately attracted to her tail band. The male stepped forward and all the scorpions immediately hissed fiercely.

John heard a soft, ease, cackle of laughter from the female scorpion. Goosebumps rose from John's arms.

"Dear, you think I will let you go that easily? You could be a tasty treat to my daughters." The scorpion beckoned at all the smaller scorpions. They all bowed their heads gracefully. John looked back at the female scorpion. She was clapping her hands in a rhythmic pattern like morse code.

The male clapped his hands twice.

John was shivering.

John wanted to pee in his pants.

John was screaming in his head.

John didn't want to go near the scorpions. He could imagine his future already as the scorpions closed in. He didn't want them but they came in like an unwanted villager. John tried to stop them but they had already knocked the door down and strangled John. yellow spots filled John's vision as thoughts came bursting in.

BAM, John dies at age 19 from a giant scorpion bite.

BAM, John dies at age 19 from shock.

BAM, John dies at age 19, goes into a coma and never wakes up again.

BAM, John dies at age 19 from accidentally banging his butt on the scorpions shells.

BAM, John dies at age 19, as he was buried in sand by a couple hundred scorpions.

John was shivering, his teeth were chattering and John's breathing was shallow. He wouldn't give up. He couldn't. Scorpions were closing in and they watched John with their stingers up. Each stinger had a small poisonous drop at the tip. The queen and king were hissing in a rhythmic *thump tumpedy thump thump*. The scorpions were now bouncing their tail off the ground to match the beat.

No, I can't die. Carla would be heartbroken without me.

John missed Carla. He wanted to be in his house, making cookies for her. He wanted to be right next to her, comforting her. He wanted to be training Riley with her. And most of all, he wanted to soak up her presence, to be happy in the way love made you happy. But life isn't fair and he had to deal with the scorpions.

John was definitely peeing his pants now. John felt a cold, chilling, sweat trickling down his neck.

John didn't want to go near the scorpions. He wasn't ready for attack. Even after all that training he did, none of it was for fighting. It was all for that stupid HighFli! If only… well he wasn't going to relive the incident where he got bit in the butt by a space scorpion.

"Look I'm stuck on this planet. Can you help me find my way out?" He asked, trying to sound friendly.

"Why would we do that?! It would betray our code!" The king scorpion roared with ferocious anger.

John reached into his pocket and felt a handle. John pulled it out to realize it was just his sword. *Just my sword. Wait! My sword… ?*

John pulled into stance ready for an attack. His hands were freezing, but ready.

"Hello fellow stranger and his uh, ugly panting mutt. How do you feel about being our dinner?" The king's laugh chilled John's bones to the core.

Were the scorpions really that heartless? Would they do that? John was perfectly happy remaining whole and not on a scorpion's dinner plate.

The king marched forward, and John ushered Riley off, who was yapping on the way. John had to admit he was upset but right now he seriously didn't need to add a stung dog onto his list of things to worry about.

John heard yaps from what he estimated was 30 feet away. John sighed and went back into his attacking stance. John grabbed his pickaxe in his right hand.

I'm ready, I'm ready, I'm ready, I'm READY!

In reality, John knew he wasn't ready. But when he was little his parents told him to never give up…

"John, remember to never give up. Promise me! Don't give up hope. When fear takes over, keep the hope. When doubt washes over you, show them you can do it! Promise me, my son, even when I'm gone. Nothing is impossible." Karia spoke gently. Zuko tickled baby John. John giggled and poked Karia. Karia poked baby John. Baby John giggled and grabbed a strand of his mother, Karia's hair. Karia pulled her hair down and kissed baby John. Zuko gave a worried glance at Karia. Karia looked back at Zuko and blinked tears out of her eyes. Baby John looked at them and giggled. He started squirming and Karia set down baby John. Tears filled her eyes.

"When I let go of the grass and go to the stars tonight, stay strong." Zuko patted baby John and kissed Karia.

"I am so so so sorry." Baby John blinked. "Why Momma?"

"Mommy! Wake up! Momma? Wake up Momma!"

"She's gone forever, John."

"Come at me, fear me!"

John knew the scorpions were anything but afraid. They came at John. Their creepy, scuttling sounds made John feel sick. He raised his axe and chopped at a few scorpions, using the light of the sword to blind some as well. John's confidence raised. He could do it. For his mom who left him when John was three.

For Carla's lost sister.

For them all.

The king and queen beckoned the scorpions back with their stingers.

Was that it? Did he win just like that?

The queen hissed and shook her head, "So arrogant. You must battle me and my husband."

John groaned. He definitely did not need this right now.

The scorpion queen snapped her tail back and forth with the poisonous tail wagging back and forth menacingly. Something in her expression told John that she would definitely win. Her husband on the other hand, was not much less scarier. He already had himself positioned in battle with those little beady eyes following John like he wanted John's bones for his new crown. His death stare melted right through John's soul.

John was shaking from head to toe. How in the world would he survive? He raised his sword and axe and SNAP! He realized that he had hit the shell of the queen scorpion. Blood was leaking out, but the queen paced forward like nothing had happened.

John quickly backed away.

"You can't surrender, you idiot!" The king shouted.

John raised his axe and chopped off the head of the king.

"NO!" The queen screamed in her raging mode. Anybody could tell it was her raging mode.

John was too busy thinking about the queen's raging mode that he didn't realize the queen was lunging for him.

"Ouch!"

Out of all the places to sting, why would the queen sting him on the butt? She had a death wish.

Without thinking, John raised his axe and threatened to hurt the queen by making exaggerated gestures. All the minor scorpions gasped.

Someone whispered, "Dude, the naked human being is threatening our queen!"

John raised his sword and flung it right in the middle of the queen's chest. It made a soft thud when it hit its target, and even John couldn't believe the accuracy of his throw.

Everyone gasped.

The queen roared with agony. She screamed and moved around in circles."You won this time but we will meet again, human being!"

John jumped up in delight. He flexed his muscles too, just for good measure. But now John was starting to feel really homesick. He didn't notice the minor scorpions creeping up on him.

Uh oh, John thought.

John pulled out his sword, hand trembling, and gripped. The sword was shaking and so was John. John gripped it tighter. He closed his eyes. John swung the sword blindly. He heard the kachink of the sword slicing a scorpion in half. John opened his eyes and spotted the queen scorpion lying on the sand.

John felt pride since the first time he came to this deadly planet. He was sure his father would have been proud. But His father wasn't there anymore. And how in the heck world was he supposed to get back to his perfect planet? His Highfli had crashed and was going to explode any second now.

BOOM!

"There it goes now…" John mumbled. What a disappointment. Okay, now he was for sure stuck on this planet forever. What an even bigger disappointment. And then Riley came to him, limping again. The Highfli explosion had hurt Riley's paw. What an even BIGGER disappointment. John quickly rummaged through his things, finding some bandages for Riley's paw. He wrapped the delicate paw up in a quick motion, and stalked off to find the perfect place to get some rest.

Chapter 4

John felt something squishy and furry. John opened up his eyes with ease. Normally, John's eyes felt crummy in the morning. He groaned and finally looked around at his surroundings. There were endless dunes and dunes of sand. The dunes loomed over John. They were like lumps of sand going on endless in all directions. The uneven lumps of sand were tall and giant, but if you looked at them from far away, they were half the size of John's thumb.

"Riley!" John groaned with complete annoyance. Riley stared at John with her precious little eyes, acting as if she was the best thing in the world. Which in fact, she was not, since she was sucky. Riley started digging a hole. John stared at her in confusion. He slapped his face as if saying, "You are severely stupid, you know that?"

"You mistake of a dog!" John cussed. Riley answered with a lovely bark. John answered with a kick into the sand. "Well, I'm gonna use the rest of my first aid to heal you so don't complain, okay?" John said, feeling rather mad.

John fixed up Riley's paw and they all started walking east. They began tromping along the sand and John felt thirsty. Why was he thirsty? John continued tromping in the sand. He could feel sweat trickling down his forehead. John wiped it off.

John muttered a curse word and continued walking. Riley was being awfully quiet. She wasn't her usual yapping mode. John couldn't even hear her walking behind him.

Maybe she was tired? John looked behind and heard himself gasp in surprise. Where was Riley? Did she just disappear into thin air? John searched and stood in terror. There was no trace of her in the vast land of sand. Where was she? John couldn't even see her footprints. John pinched himself. Maybe he was dreaming. Thank god he was. Riley was happily tromping behind in her Yapp mode.

"YAPPPP!" she barked. John let out a sigh of relief. Although John desperately did not want her to be in her Yappy mode.

"YAPPY!" Riley barked again. John gave Riley a light slap on the forehead. He would persist through the dark. John tramped along the sandy and gritty sand. He looked around carefully and inspected the sand. John saw light acorn shaped footprints. Someone else had been here. Probably some other alien. That didn't really bother John.

John felt desperately thirsty so he took a very long sip of water. John let out a breath and raised his arm to wipe his mouth. John's lips felt dry. How long had he been on this planet anyway? Why was he here? Why couldn't he use his mighty Jakulan powers to break free from this prison? Questions John should have asked himself earlier flooded his head.

John set down his backpack. He was a bit tired. Johns slowly reached into his backpack for the only amount of water left. John looked at the wimpy, dirty, and brown water. John chugged it all down. It tasted audacious and murky. John almost wanted to spit it out. One minute it was clean and the next minute it was gross. John was beginning to think that the quality of his belongings were pretty low.

It didn't matter now. John pulled out his book of quotes from his backpack. "Life is really simple, but we insist on making it complicated." *I wish my life could be simple. Why would I complicate it?* John wondered. "Who every wrote this is stupid." John yelled, "STUPID! Plain down STUPID! It doesn't even make any sense!" John felt anger boil inside of him. Boiling and angry, John tried to calm down.

John attempted to reason with himself. "So if my life was simple then i would be a chicken and my whole life goal is to sit there and lay eggs…. But i am not a chicken and how is that my fault!?" John yelled at himself, "How did I complicate it!?" John then understood the meaning. " I could have stayed at my house and trained Riley. Instead I had to complicate things with my obsessions and greed." John understood now. He then simply sat down and slept until the morning.

Now John had been traveling for a long time and was weary. He began hallucinating. John looked over his shoulder and started yelping like Riley. John began to realize he was getting really thirsty. It was getting dark and he had to find some water. The only problem? He couldn't find any. The thirst was like there was a clawing snail trying to poison and claw its way out.

John shuddered. He remembered being poisoned by a clawing snail. They HURT. It felt like someone was stabbing a poisoned knife right in the middle of his neck.

He sat down on the sand and sighed. He paused for a moment and watched the stars. They were so bright and pretty. Maybe they could tell him how to get home or at least water. He groaned. He walked towards the place with most stars and just watched them.

He knew he was getting thirsty but the stars reminded him so much of Carla. He tried to touch them. He shook himself.

No John thought. He had to find the water. Water was the need.

John walked around wondering if there was water even on this planet. He saw some weird looking creatures. Under closer inspection, he realized that they were simply just asian elephants. The giant gray creatures blasted their trunks. They flopped their giant ears often as they walked. There was a tiny elephant hiding behind a giant elephant in the front.

Wait! John realized. If asian elephants could survive here, then there must have been water. He followed the elephants.

After a few hours of depressing thirst, he saw it, a pond! It was crystal blue with glittering sunshine glinting off of it.

This was exactly what he needed. Fresh spring water. He took it in his hands and drank it. It was the best thing John could ever imagine. Nice soothing fresh spring water. Almost as beautiful as his Highfli. Probably more. He grabbed a big bottle of water from the car crash. The water would last about a month. Maybe even more if John didn't drink too much of it. He filled it all the way to the top with nice, fresh, cooling spring water. It was just so refreshing. John felt water slowly trickling down his neck as John chugged it all down. John used his arm to wipe off the water still left on the edge of his mouth.

John took his bottle of water and filled it to the top again. John looked down at the crystal clear water.

He bet Carla would love to swim in it. In fact, John hated swimming but just looking at this made him want to. He chugged down some more water. John remembered that he and Carson used to see who could chug more water. Carson always won. John just didn't have the skills. Carson was probably half bullfrog or something. John used to be jealous of Carson but now he didn't even care! This water was just perfect. He wishes he could just have it all to himself. But it was time to get going now. He walked past the colorful violet sunset and sighed. If only Carla were here to watch it with him. That would have been wonderful. But John was far away from home. In fact, he might never come home ever again.

He felt tears seep out of his eyes. He grabbed a cushion from the Highfli crash and slept through the wonderful dazzling night. John looked at the dazzling stars. John thought about all that had happened since John came to planet Dead. The scorpion invasion, finding his dad, and sandstorm. John got tired. He blinked once, then twice, then John fell asleep. In his dreams John thought of his dog Riley yapping around.

Suddenly, Riley disappeared and John leaned over a railing and saw Riley flailing helplessly in the raging wind. She was going to fall in the sea! And there were hundreds of orcas and Hammerheads and Great White sharks, all swimming and waiting for Riley to be in their mouth. John's mouth became sour. "Riley!" John yelled. John panicked and threw his sword down. "Riley, float on the sword!" John yelled but he knew it was helpless. Riley would keep falling no matter what. As time slowed down, John seemed to watch the world end. "Riley!" John shouted. "You're gonna make it! I believe in you!" John had to stop himself from jumping over the railing. What would happen if John jumped over the railing with Riley? Then, Riley came soaring up and over the railing with John's sword in her mouth. But that dream didn't last long. John's dreams became his nightmares as he thought about how he probably would die on this planet and how Carla would die trying to find him. John wanted to reunite, not die. Would that actually happen in reality though? John started getting dizzy from the thought, and then everything went black.

Chapter 5

John woke up with a start. Immediately John realized there were several flaws in waking up. 1, John's eyes felt weirdly crummy. 2, John immediately fell back down. So much for waking up.

"What time is it, Carla?" He moaned. *Wait.* John realized. *Where was he?* Oh yeah, stupid him. He was on a you-are-going-to- die-planet. He looked around. *Hmmm,* he wondered, *what did he need now?* John marched up a giant sand dune and saw big dents everywhere. *Hmmm...* John thought again. He looked over his shoulder, nothing. John felt really lonely these days. It was 3 days since the scorpion attack. John's butt had almost healed completely. John wondered if that was normal. He followed the dents in the sand until he realized it was the prints of a big bear.

He checked to make sure there was no danger around and continued following the tracks. He followed it all day. John felt the weight of the sun on his back. The pounding star was smack in the middle of the sky. The sun was pretty and all, but it was extremely hot. Its bright rays spread over the vast, dry desert. John kept on following the large bear tracks.

John froze. Panic was rising in his chest. Was it just his imagination or was there a snake slithering around in the sands. John had only glimpsed a giant long snake with a black mouth. John froze, trying to keep still and at the same time, trying to spot a long slithering line. John's eyes popped out. There, behind a small cactus lay a giant snake, silvery gray on the top but with the underside scales of pure white. The snake hadn't yet realized John might be a possible threat. It was too busy attacking a small brown mouse. The mouse had no ability that it could use to defend itself against the giant snake. John watched silently as the snake lunged toward the helpless rodent. Two long white fangs sank into the back of the rodent. Until he was stopped by a bear.

"What do you think you are doing here?" barked a very big bear with devil horns and really large claws.

"Umm, n-n-n-nothing" John stammered frantically. He did not need this bear to be a part of his life. John really wanted to run away or scream but that would be weird. Plus the bears would just kill him.

So he replied once again,"Actually, can you give me an introduction about your kind?"

"Why yes." The bear explained that they were Big Bears and bears were descended from them. He also explained they were the best animals ever and so ancient that they were around when there were Dodo Birds. John was actually fascinated but he decided not to say that.

Apparently Big bears were very fond of themselves. Extremely fond of themselves. They also forced John to go to their city.

John walked around into their village. Nobody seemed surprised that John was there. In fact they all acted like it happened everyday. Which was probably not true. John was sent to meet the queen and king of the Big bears and they were not nice.

"We should execute him."

"I think he should eat him."

"I want to kill him."

John shivered. This was not what he had expected. "What have I done wrong?" John asked nervously.

"EVERYTHING!" The queen yelled at him. Now this was worse, way worse than a raging mode scorpion queen.

John felt scared. And so empty too. He missed Carla and Carson. And he forgot Riley!

Uh, oh. John thought. The queen bear kicked him out into the busy city. He thought it wouldn't be bad but John was wrong. Big bears threw things at him and yelled bad curse words too. He saw a muddy dog with familiar eyes walk by being yelled at by a Big bear.

Wait, that is Riley. How did she get there?

"Hey," John yelled. "That is my pet."

"That's convenient," Snarled the bear, "She is so annoying."

Someday I'm going to start a factory that makes bear killer. John thought. The Bear's claws measured six inches. John had taken classes on how to measure even with no ruler. John felt like he just betrayed Riley.

When he wasn't paying attention, Riley had snuck away to find food. Now that John thought about it, he felt like Riley had betrayed him.

While John was daydreaming, the bear's claws hooked into his arm. The sharp tips of the claws scratched at him over and over again. It cut open a huge wound, but suddenly, a shape emerged from the darkness. The bear howled in pain as the bone-white teeth of Riley the dummy sunk into the bear's shoulder. John took the chance and threw his sword at the bear's head. The bear howled one last scream of pure savageness, then flopped to the side, dead. Fortunately, all the other bears were too frightened to fight John.

As the bear fell, one of its claws pulled off John's undies. John quickly pulled them back on. John led Riley to a nearby waterfall. The water was crystal-clear and really loud.

There, he took a bath, and made Riley hold a cloth in front of him so that aliens couldn't spot him. Riley, who did not like to obey commands, threw the cloth on a wet rock to let it dry out.

"Riley!" John shrieked. John did not like being naked, without cover. Riley looked over at John, blinking innocent eyes. Angel eyes from Riley were the most annoying. Riley almost laughed. She let out a happy yip and ran off. "RIley!" John yelled. Riley was very bad at obeying commands or orders. She normally didn't follow orders at all. Unless you gave her treats with the order. Then Riley would follow the order and overdo the order.

For instance, one time, John came out into his lawn to cut some grass down because the grass was growing crazy. It was almost as tall as Riley, who was extremely tall for a golden retriever, in fact, Riley was as tall as a male Great Dane. Those things were huge. John used to own one. The Great Dane was nearly as tall as Carla, only a head shorter. When Riley had run through John's lawn, she'd disappeared with the tall golden grass. John had taken hours to find her. He felt it would have been much easier if she had just followed his orders.

Another time, when John was little, He'd climbed a tree and couldn't get down. John told Baby Riley to go fetch his father and instead, Riley had come back with a twig. John had then jumped off the tree and fallen. John had ordered Riley to bark as loud as she could so John's dad could come out. Instead, Riley started sniffing John's wound and licked it. When John's father finally came out, John could not explain why there was dog spit covering him.

From a lot of John's memories in general, Riley was the worst at following rules. John didn't know what was wrong with her brain. Honestly, John didn't even know if she had a brain at all. John was concerned for RIley's well being. Very concerned. John was afraid that when RIley died , she might be missing an ear or tail because she died from trying to bite it off.

Nonetheless, John got out of the stream, and tugged the shirt from a rock up high. John slammed on the shirt and immediately got it wet but he didn't care. John frowned. There wasn't any way that Riley could put the T-Shirt up there , the rock was too high for her unless… unless… unless she didn't even put it there.

Chapter 6

Possibly snakes? Giant Wendigos? John at least wanted a chance to fight back. John remembered one of the quotes from his book, "Life is tough so get tougher." John needed to be tough. But how?

John attempted to run away hoping the bears wouldn't see him but they did and one of the bears said, "Come here."

With a jolt, John realized it was the queen. John quickly ran over to a little shrub and put it in front of himself and huddled.

"I am not blind, I can see you," Battle Scar yelled.

John didn't know why he knew that her name was Battle Scar but his sensitive mind could tell that. John slowly moved behind the shrub to the right and at the last moment when no one was looking John dashed off behind the tree and climbed it. This was NOT easy.

1. John had only climbed small trees, not big trees from other planets.

2. He had promised Carla never to climb trees and as a Witcher Carla enchanted him so that climbing trees would be hard. And as a Jokula John easily deflected the spell but guiltiness crept inside him. John hid at the top of the tree hoping he wouldn't be seen.

"Sharp Claw, find the alien."

Alien? John thought. *You're the aliens here.* John thought. But it made sense, he was an outsider. John was so busy thinking about this, he didn't notice a big bear with extremely sharp claws. Sharp Claw. John thought instinctively. John raised his axe and whisper shouted,

"I can kill you any time now,"

John put one end of the blade against the bear's neck.

"In your dreams, alien," The bear snorted.

The bear picked John up and carried him off to the place across from the queen. They had set up a little square there that read,"The place across from the queen."

John braced himself for battle and the bear held up a picture of John and snarled," Is this you? One of our guards found this human in the desert near a pile of metal."

John froze. It was him with clothes all right. "N-N-No s-sir." John stammered. John felt ominous. It felt like he had pneumonoultramicroscopicsilicovolcanoconiosis (it's a disease from inhaling volcanic ash and sulfur). John barfed out some sand. It was gross.

"Bleh." John spat out.

"So unkingly." The queen muttered.

John sighed. This queen would be tough. "I challenge you." The queen cried.

Uh oh… John thought. John positioned himself remembering moves that his Karate teacher and fencing teacher had taught. *Right hand to underbelly swipe* John thought as the queen, Battle Scar lunged at him, belly exposed. He dodged a swipe and a lung and he attacked both gracefully and swiftly and fast. It all happened in a blur until the queen fought out the words,

"You win, kill me and take my hide, I have underestimated you." Battle Scar growled graciously.

John took a deep breath and with effort, stabbed the queen in the heart. He shaved off her fur and skin and put the face of the queen on his head. Truthfully, John felt bad for the queen. He kind of wished that he could know the queen better. He buried every part except the hide in a lush part of grass covered in flowers. He grabbed a stone and carved out a message with his knife.

John sighed.

He walked away and strode into the city.

It just happened that the bear king, Battle Winner was there. John huddled up hoping he wouldn't be spotted. "I will get you back, little alien," Battle Winner stated very angrily, obviously in *his* rage mode. John got ready for attack until he realized that King Battle Winner was simply standing over his wife's body. King Battle Winner had a lot of jewelry. There was a thick, long, chainmail around his throat as well as a bedazzled crown with flicks of silver across Battle Winner's back. Battle Winner had a diamond-encrusted in his forehead and tiny rubies encrusted on the tips of his eyes.

Battle Winner also had a circle of diamonds around his short, ruby-covered tail.

Battle Winner looked more like a Jewelry Winner instead of a Battle Winner but John had seen Battle Winner's claws. Like the rest of his body, Battle Winner had diamond-covered claws but they were stained with dark red blood. His claws were extra long and sharp. As if hearing John's thoughts, Battle Winner suddenly lunged toward John's bush. John's last thought was " I am gonna get killed by a giant bear with diamonds covering him."

John awoke, but only in his dreams. John turned around and saw a Casoli, a female, with glowing blue markings. She had her back turned to him. She was reading a book. When John walked closer to her, she finally looked at John. She was really pretty and had that intense and serious expression. John had a feeling that this was her normal expression. John had a feeling that she looked like Carla, only a Casoli with some Jokulan scales on the tips of her eyes. Her eyes intensified and narrowed at John. "What are you doing here?" She barked. Her voice sounded angry but with a hint of confusion.

John stuttered "I - I j-j-just ended u-up h-here in my d-d-dreams...?" To John, his statement sounded more like a question than a fact. "Are you sure? You don't sound sure. You're not supposed to end up in my dreams. After all, it is my dream, not yours. I get to control what's happening."

The girl tapped her chin a few times, thinking through. Or at least John thought, her expression seemed the same.

"Of course I am thinking, you dingus!" She snapped then shut her mouth. How did she know what John thought?

Well, she's weird.

The girl looked mystified. "Weird how?" she asked. "W-what do y-you mean...?" John stuttered. How had she read his thoughts?

"Weird power I have. Sorry if it's disturbing," the girl replied glumly.

Just what I need. John thought silently, *a mind reader.*

The girl seemed hurt by John's thoughts. She glanced down at her hands and shook her head like she didn't want to cry.

"Sorry! I can't help it!" She spoke, her voice trembling and her hands shaking.

John suddenly awoke from sleep, the girl disappearing from his vision. In front of him, beady red eyes stared John down.

Chapter 7

"HELP," John shrieked, terrified by the beady red eyes piercing John's own blue eyes. But of course, the aliens were all scared of bears, except one. Someone with dark tan skin and black spiky hair crept out.

The alien's name was Frank. Out in the tan haze of the desert, Frank saw a flare and hopped on his hoverbike. The hoverbike was a combination of a bike and a hoverboard; it looked like a flying motorcycle.

Back at Frank's house, Frank's mom was panicking a little, wondering where Frank was. His dinner was getting cold. Turns out, Frank had just landed at the bear's prison.

He quickly located John, sitting in the jail cell, hands touching the rusty bars. Frank told John to hush because he was going to use a laser mine to blast the jail cell apart. John was given a spear and grenades. Since Frank had spare spears, he gave them to John.

"Alright, let's go," Frank said, "use your spear to fend off bears." As they reached the main courtyard, about a hundred bears were there.

"Ooh, the pathetic prisoner has a little friend. I guess we'll eat both of them, then. Ooh Haha, mwahaha, Bwaahaha!" (more evil laughter). John and Frank looked around. Bears circled them everywhere.

Suddenly, someone shouted, "Hey, look who you are messing with!" It was a Casoli—a Jokula but with light blue skin that glowed, blue hair that glowed, marks on the hips, wrists, and ankles that were blue and glowing especially bright and their breed also tended to have marks under their eyes and antennae. That obviously meant she was an important role.

"Get out!" She yelled while throwing a blade at a massive bear. John ran for his dear rear end's life along with Frank. John quickly found a hiding spot in a hole behind the wall. John sat there for AGES, his palms sweat already creating pools on the ground. Finally after what seemed like ages the tarp opened.

"Come on, do you want to get caught?" John obediently followed.

Frank shook his head "How can we trust you?"

"You can't, so STAY here instead and get killed."

"Fine." Frank stamped his foot.

"Well my name is Aspen Jasper."

"Ooh!" John said, "My girlfriend's name is Carla Jasper!"

Aspen looked shocked but then she nodded. She pointed down an alley.

UM SORRY THIS IS John's thoughts, right? That's not an alley, it's a hallway. John, learn your grammar. Now I'm taking over for the rest of the chapter. Shoo shoo. But- too bad John. Anyway. **AHEM.**

I led Frank and John down the hallway and John had a fuming expression on his face. I **TOTALLY** *don't know why. We crept up and I ushered the boys to hide behind the corner. Then the stupidest idea came to my mind. I ran into plain sight. Some guards followed behind me. I gulped. I pulled up my hoodie and took out my daggers.*

I muttered an enchantment under my breath, "OH EIXN DIJNIJ IJNFKD." I chanted. The daggers blazed to life. I turned around and jumped and tackled down a guard. I swung my knife on his bare neck and sadly, cut off his head. I swung my knife around and around till all the bears were dead.

Do you hear that John? I'm better than you! I ran into the nearest room and hid there. And then I muttered a spell to teleport to John and Frank. They were utterly surprised. Just kidding. They expected me to be back soon so they were utterly mad. Yup, that's just how annoying I am.

John ran, following Aspen and she muttered something under her breath.

"It's a spell she told us." Frank blinked in surprise. They didn't notice the giant bear that was behind us. Suddenly John blacked out. John woke up with a start. All around him was darkness.

"Hello?" John asked.

"Hi dude." Aspen's voice replied. John looked in the direction of the voice, finding Aspen's face that was painted with annoyance. She looked like a human beacon. John giggled uncontrollably.

Aspen pouted. "You would be grumpy too if YOU were glowing."

"But I'm not!" John snorted. Aspen glared at John.

John snorted *like a pig. Ha! Gotcha back. And WHY AM I STILL GLOWING?.*

John began pushing the buttons and pulling out plugs on the walls. The plugs and buttons kept popping out everywhere. John could feel it. 2 minutes later, the light was on. John looked around. There were 2 doors.

"What?" A voice called from behind John.

John leaped out of his scales. *Oh, It's just Frank. Whew. I thought it would be a bear.* John instructed Aspen to go through the door on the right. He and Frank would be going through the door on the left. It was time to split up and take the challenge. He and Frank stepped out both holding their tongues.

"Uh oh, looks like someone is in trouble!" a bear shouted. John and Frank bolted away. They met another group of Special Ops bears, each holding a giant knife and a wicked-looking rifle. John and Frank barely managed to duck behind cover A the bears opened fire, bullets slamming into the wall behind them. John searched the floor for a gun, threw his spear at one bear, and picked up a rifle. John peeked out of cover, then started firing his machine gun. Bears fell in pools of blood as the bullets streaked through the air and embedded themselves in the bears. The bears fell back and dove for cover, too. One of the bears fired a bullet from its rifle, nearly hitting John.

One of the bears was carrying a special knife, its blade glowing with white symbols. John leaned around his cover and fired. A flash of purple streaked through the air, the bear falling mere seconds later. John kept moving, Frank right behind him. Rounding a corner, John saw another group of bears. The bears were looting a dead body, one of them slitting open clothes while slicing through the skin as well. John threw a grenade, and he saw all the bears lying in the middle of the room, the walls splattered with gory stuff. John and Frank walked carefully through the bloody mess, occasionally stopping to see if they had stepped on anything. The building opened up into a wide corridor, bears guarding a door in the far wall. Riley came sauntering in with a piece of the bear gut in her mouth, looking very happy. The bears charged, raising their guns with bayonets attached, seeming intent on stabbing John, Frank, and Riley. Riley flung her piece of the bear gut at one of the bears, the bear slipping on the gross intestine.

John shot the bear, then grabbed the bayonet and flung it at the other bear. The bayonet thunked into the bear's stomach, the bear doubling over in pain. John took the other bear's bayonet, then shot the moaning bear. John took out the bayonet from the bear's belly, then continued forward through the door. Inside was a huge bear, standing five feet tall with dual blades. John shot rapidly, bullets flying through the air in a stream. The bullets hit the bear, who just stood there, smiling. It was at this moment that John knew this was going to be a long fight.

The first few hours were boring. John had fired at least 350 shots, and the bear was only critically injured. Three hundred fifty shots were enough to take down 350 bears, yet it didn't even take down one. The bear stood there, seeming very relaxed. Suddenly, it whipped out a rifle. John and Frank dived behind cover as bullets whizzed over their heads. John threw a bayonet, and it thunked into the bear's head. But the bear only flinched, showing no sign of pain. More bullets were generated inside the rifle and were spewed out immediately. All the expensive ceramic pots, urns, and vases in the room were shattered. John turned the power knob to "max" on his gun and then fired a bear bullet.

The bullet slammed into the bear with enough strength that it could have made a SandWorm double over in agony, but it just knocked the bear off its feet instead. The bear clutched at what was obviously a bleeding wound, then got back up and started firing again. John crouched behind a table, but the bear's rifle shredded the table and almost hit John in the butt. John crouched behind an enormous geode, knowing that the rock was very thick and would offer wonderful protection. John peeked out of cover, fired, then ducked back behind cover as fifteen bullets slammed into the wall behind him. The bullets shredded a painting, bits of cloth hanging off of the wall. A smoking bullet flew out of the gun. John peeked around to see a hole in the bear's side, and what looked like… a bullet-proof vest?!

John shouted for Frank to cover him as he sprang out of cover and reached for the bit of exposed bullet-proof vest. He yanked it out, and the bear ran behind cover as well. The bear peeked around the cover, only to be hit by John's bullet. He regenerated another one and walked over to the bear. The bear lay crumpled on the ground, blood pooling on the polished wooden floor. The floor was littered with bits of ceramic shards and splinters.

John ran out of the room, Frank hot on his heels. They ran right into a patrol of bears...

Chapter 8

"Oh, an alien. I think we'll soon be tasting alien meat, but the main course will be man and dog."

The bear said with a terrifying cackle that chilled John. The bear was about 10 feet tall and had awfully sharp claws, which were sharp enough to pierce John. The bear was insanely tall in comparison to John's tiny figure. Its shadow was at least 20 feet.

BANG, BANG!

Frank and John's rifle shots quickly hit the bear in unison. John put himself into position, ready for bear attacks but was quickly stopped by Frank.

"Stop, we're going to make it worse." Frank said, seeming like he was choosing his words carefully.

He grabbed John's hand and dragged him back inside the room through the door they had come from.

"We must go to the base's basement." Frank whispered. "My scanners told me that there is a box of frag grenades in there. We should be able to get our hands on those, and then blow our way out. It's going to be loud and dangerous, so take a shield and earplugs. You probably want to keep your ears attached to your head."

They were able to sneak past guards, thanks to John's rifle. Once in the basement, Frank pulled out a flashlight, illuminating the surroundings. Not only was there a box of grenades, but there was also a pickaxe and a crate. It was like a little treasure chest of death.

John, having found a pickaxe, easily reduced the dark oak crate to splinters. Inside, there were more grenades and food and utensils

John used the pickaxe to hit the ground and make a hole, then Frank planted the grenade in the hole. *BOOM!* The grenades and landmines easily carved out large swaths of dirt. *BOOM, BOOM, BOOM!* They carved out a tunnel to the surface. There, a large group of angry-looking bears were waiting.

"GET OVER HERE!" The bears shouted angrily. John and Frank panicked and John shot his rifle at the bears and killed one of them. Frank then used his rifle to dispatch the others. However, there was one bear that had gleaming iron armor, and had a gun, too. It quickly became one of those ghost town gun fights that were in the movies John watched. After half an hour, they were still battling it out, the bear with about five hundred holes in his iron armor, hiding behind a telephone pole, and John and Frank, hiding behind big rocks and reloading.

One hour later, the ground was littered with bullet shells and scraps of iron armor. The rocks were badly cracked, and the telephone pole was just a shot away from splintering into pieces. John peeped from his hiding place and fired. The bear cried out in pain as the bullet hit his chest. With sudden rage, the bear fired the entire load of bullets in his gun, and ran behind a wall to reload. John and Frank gained on him, going one rock closer. John threw a throwing knife and splintered the telephone pole. There was a loud crackling as the pole fell, electric particles dancing on the wiring. The bear had finished reloading his huge rifle, and he fired another shot at the cracked rock. The rock exploded into shards of tiny rock.

Five hours later, the pressure was still on. John was almost out of bullets, and the landscape looked as if it had been stuck by an airstrike. The bear was limping with dark blood dripping from its arm and foot, and John's leg was wrapped up in ace wrap. Frank was still shooting like a maniac, and John was tending to his wound. The bear was crouched behind a very broken shed, and

Frank and John were hiding behind gigantic iron bars. The iron had several dents, and everyone's gun barrels were glowing red hot and smoking. John was shooting his 157th bullet, and finally killed the bear. John's face was sweating, and Frank was trying to unjam his rifle. John and Frank had two Slurm sodas and a bacon cheeseburger each for dinner, then headed out of the city. There were guards, but John's sledgehammer quickly gave them a big bonk on the head and spoke good night to them. John and Frank were tired, too, so they walked into an inn with a sign that said, "The Bear Den" and slept there. The following morning, the innkeeper, Mr. FluffyFur, offered them a classic breakfast (for bears) with minced meat, wild berries, and a classic bear smoothie which I don't even want to describe because it was so gross. So, Frank and John ordered Cofe instead. It used to be spelled coffee, but the Jolukan government changed it to Cofe, since who would waste time writing an extra "e" and an extra "f"?

They bought some bullets and a pint of ale, then left the inn. Right outside, a heavily armed bear was waiting with dual revolvers. He had reinforced iron armor, and challenged John and Frank to a duel.

"I heard that you defeated the bear general in only six hours and thirty minutes. I am his boss, and I challenge you to a duel!" the bear grumbled/shouted. The bear hid behind a large wall, and John and Frank also hid behind walls. The Bear Commander totally trashed his dual revolvers and pulled out the rifle from his backpack. Shooting five bullets per second, John and Frank were actually afraid to come out. But then, John squeezed off a perfect shot and cracked the reinforced iron. The bear reloaded, and John threw his last hand grenade at the bear's hiding spot. Then it was all over in a split second. The blinding flash of the grenade, the deafening roar of the boom, and the chips of reinforced iron all over the ground.

John generated another bullet, and moved on. Around another corner, the Bear King pulled out a machine gun and started firing. John ducked behind a rock just as bullets slammed into a telephone line. The king had ornate armor that only showed the smallest of cracks when one of John's bullets hit it. John put on the bulletproof vest from the other bear, and marched out. John charged forward, strapping the rifle to his back. He snatched the King Bear's rifle, but it was pretty much the same as his own rifle. John sprinted back, but the King bear pulled out a pistol and fired. Several bullets grazed John's arm and legs, but he managed to make it back to cover safely. The King Bear kept firing, but the bullets just hit the rock. John fired his rifle,

John ran off the street, and realized that the big road he was on has gun barrels poking out of windows in the houses. He dove into a small shed just as a thousand bullets slammed into the street like metal hail. John snuck into a house, as Frank snuck into another. John killed the bear with a quick bayonet stab, then ran out of the house. Another gun barrel poked out of the remaining houses as Frank ran out of the house he was in. John threw a grenade through one of the houses' windows and the second story erupted into a ball of fire, with wood splinters and bits of brick raining down onto the street.

Frank threw a grenade as well, and more wooden splinters and brick bits showered onto the street. John aimed at one of the gun barrels, but before he could fire, a stream of bullets slammed into his chest, shredding the last bit of the bulletproof vest. John dove behind a ruined building's wall as a bullet slipped past him. John shot one bear, but it wasn't enough. John threw a grenade. An entire house exploded as the grenade tore through the walls and killed the bears inside.

Frank charged into a house, rifle tearing through bear armor and punching a neat hole in each body. John grabbed a rifle and charged in, bullets flying as he shot down bear after bear, the animals falling like sliced wheat. He fired shot after shot, gun barrels disappearing from the windows rapidly. But then, one of the gun barrels was replaced with a tip of a rocket, pointed straight at John! He rushed out of the building just as a rocket explosion tore apart the building. John and Frank charged into the rocket launcher building, trailed closely by ten bullets per second. John made it into the building and shot down the bear. John was running low on bullets, so they strapped their rifles to their backs and ran out of the city.

Chapter 9

After they escaped the bear city, John saw someone out in the haze. They thought it was Carla, but they were not sure.

Frank fired his rifle into the air. The bullet made a whistling sound as it cut through the thick air. Frank then threw a spear into the haze with a handwritten note.

Dear person,

Please go the way the sword's handle was pointing. There you will find John and me. I am a friend of John's but I am not Jolukan. Please help us, and then John and you can fly back home.

Sincerely,

Frank, John's alien friend

After Frank threw the spear, John distributed slightly burnt and melted snacks to several small gooey creatures, a sand spirit, Frank, and himself. The small goey creatures jumped on the cookies with their slimy, green feet. The cookies broke up into pieces, and then the creatures ate the crumbs. The sand spirit ate the cookie in one gulp. Apparently, John had displaced one of the snacks, because he didn't have one for himself.

Suddenly, a towering form emerged from the thick dust. The smell of a cigar and gunpowder filled the air as Ophelia the Outlaw hopped off of her own Highfli. She introduced herself to John and Frank and she pulled out her huge shotgun. She also pulled out a giant crate of the finest steak. John and Frank's eyes widened and their mouths started drooling.

A few seconds later, Frank and John have bits of steak on their faces as they continue to stuff the meat into their mouths. Splinters of the crate's lid were lying in the sand. That night, while John and Frank were sleeping, Ophelia splashed a weakness potion on Frank. Her plan was going well. Then, Ophelia's walkie talkie crackled. Ophelia ran away from where John and Frank were sleeping and listened.

"Ophelia, come in. Are you there?" the captain of Ophelia's outlaw squadron asked.

Ophelia nodded in a sort of regal like manner.

"I'm just checking in to see how the plan is going. Is everything in place?"

"It's going great. I have acquired my first target!"

"That's acceptable to hear, but remember what we taught you in trainee school. Put your progress in percentages."

Ophelia knew she didn't really have much in ways of progress. "Only about five percent or so, but I promise I'm getting there," she muttered.

"WHAT?! ONLY FIVE PERCENT? Ophelia, you need to work faster!"

"Yeah but I need to wait for the perfect opportunity to kidnap my target!"

"Okay, fine, but hurry up!" the captain shouted vigorously.

And then there was silence. Ophelia considered what her boss had said, and then she looked back at John and Frank. Her mind worked out a plan, but it was a difficult one. She planned out all the details of how to kidnap Frank, and thought about the dangers and rewards. Was it worth the risk?

The next morning, John and Frank awoke to Ophelia snoring very loudly on the empty steak crate which had been flipped over. Frank tried to get up, but felt surprisingly heavy. John carried Frank onto Ophelia's Highfli.

Sadly, Ophelia's Highfli wasn't powerful enough to fly back to Joluka. John tried to go upwards, but just crashed in the sand. John tried again, and failed again. John tried 128 more times, but failed 128 times. John looked in his Little Book of Quotes.

"Know thy self, know thy enemy. A thousand battles, a thousand victories." -Sun Tzu

"Well, Sun Tzu, I like your quote, but right now I know myself, I know the Highfli, so why do I try to get this darn thing up into the sky a thousand times, but fail a thousand times?" John asked himself. John took out his pocketknife, which he always kept in his pocket, and cut a few wires here and there, and tried again. John instantly regretted this, since the Hightfli exploded. Fortunately, John had really fast reflexes from video games that he played when he was young, so he pulled Frank and himself out just in time. Unfortunately, Ophelia woke up. When she saw that her life savings had been ruined, she instantly grabbed her shotgun and started a major battle with John and Frank. Frank was still too weak to grab a gun, so John did the fighting. Ophelia had a rifle, and John still had his rifle. The arena was a half-sunken city, and there were many surprises that were about to be discovered…

The second the battle started, a Giant Scorpion rose from the ruins. Ophelia and John called a temporary truce in order to kill the scorpion. Ophelia's gun proved to be stronger than it seemed, with expanding fat metal pieces that drove into the scorpion's flesh, and then exploded into tiny bits of shrapnel. John's rifle shot big fat fast bullets that made nasty wounds. Within a few minutes, the scorpion died and Ophelia opened fire on John. John ducked behind a big stone, and Ophelia stood on a big tower. John shot at Ophelia, and hit her boot. But still, the bullet made a big wound. Ophelia shot back down, but only hit John's rock. Ophelia surrendered after 2 hours of back-and-forth shooting, and they signed a little armistice, meaning that both people would stop firing. They walked off into the haze, and Ophelia's plan was going as planned.

Two hours of walking in the desert later, Ophelia's walkie-talkie buzzed again.

"Yes, chief?"

"How's the progress going?"

"30%"

The captain let out a long sigh, and said, "Ophelia, I am giving you 72 hours, and if you don't finish by then, I am sending you off, which let me remind you, means you're fired."

"Yes, sir."

"OK then, you shall return with the hostage at 12 A.M. on Sunday."

As Ophelia considered what she would do, she pulled out the Ghost Poison dagger. The dark metal made a sharp sound as it came out of the sheath. John heard the sound, and pulled out his cutlass. Ophelia took the chance when John wasn't looking, and stabbed him in the back. The Ghost Poison sunk into John's blood, and in a state of pain and shock, cut off Ophelia's right hand that was holding the dagger. But the damage had been done, and John was now in an uncomfortable position, too. Ophelia's left hand was missing, John had a stab wound in his back, and Frank was under a weakness spell.

Ophelia's hand was missing, so she had one hand to do things that required two hands. And since John and Frank didn't trust her, she had no one to help. Just to improve the mood, Ophelia's one-of-a-kind pet rat had died at her gang's HQ.

After the incident, Frank and John now had serious trust issues. They would not even trust a little cute, ten eyed skriph that constantly followed them around. John gave in and gave the critter a little pod of khnocile kelp.

The skriph gobbled down the kelp in a few seconds, and tripled in size. John and Ophelia quickly got their weapons out and started attacking the skriph. Ophelia fired her shotgun single-handedly, and Frank staggered as he shot his rifle. Frank wished that he could help but he was too weak to do anything at the moment. Frank summoned the energy required to throw a big clump of sticky sand into the shrimp's face, and made it back off. Frank unexpectedly saved the day with sand.

Chapter 10

John felt dizzy all day. His vision was shaking and he was walking in circles. John felt like slumping down on a couch. Problem, there weren't any couches around for John to slump down on. John turned in a circle. Yellow spots danced around his vision making him tired and thirsty. John looked behind him. Was that a … dinosaur? And a monkey rabbit with a snail head? "Carson!" John yelled with delight. Carson was standing right there with his arms open. Or was he…? John questioned himself. "Hurrrp!" John hiccuped.

What was going on? Apparently he was sick and that wasn't good. From obvious evidence. What kind of sickness did John have? Everything was very dizzy. Bad thing that Frank wasn't here to help him. Apparently his mom was making him dinner and Frank was off in a suicidal mission.

Very……..Very………..Nice. John thought. So here was John in the middle of the desert finding an important potion. And here was Frank resting lying in desert sands. John was getting sick already from that thought. John grabbed his bottle and took some baby sips which turned into huge gulps.

Suddenly, John didn't know why but he felt that something in his arm had exploded.

A little rest wouldn't hurt, I guess. John thought.

John sat down and quietly munched down on some Frobutes.

My arm really hurts now, what is wrong with me?" John thought.

Just then something happened. John's arm stung like an lightning bolt suddenly and a little place near the elbow on John's arm was turning red. It looked like the inside there was… dying. The inside quickly turned white and John's entire body jolted with pain.

Ouch. Now he had three choices:

1. Pray to the Jolukan god of medicine to expel this terrible disease from his body.

2. Amputate his arm.

3. Find medicine.

Just then, the wound began to bubble and wiggle like a giant worm. Then, a huge purple tentacle rose out of the infected section and gripped his other arm. John watched in horror as the tentacle extended a claw, ripped open his skin, and crawled in. approximately two seconds later the skin turned a pale white, the color of bone, and then started to drop off of his skeleton. The other arm was also rotting, and John could now see his ghostly white bones. He started to panic as the bone slowly turned to ashes.

Just then, someone shot a file of a mysterious lime green brew onto his bones. Instantly, flesh grew out of them, and his bones were healed. Frank emerged from the shadows, holding another solution. John tried to hug his friend, but Frank slowly pulled back.

"That potion will only heal you for 24 hours. Right now it's 3:00 pm. Tomorrow at 3:00 pm the virus will break through. I know five ruins of temples that will contain the perfect medicine: an Effect Remover potion. When Ophelia stabbed you, she inflicted the Ghost effect on you. One of the ruins should have an Effect Remover potion. These ruins are large, though. Usually, the real prizes are hidden in a secret basement. It will take the strength of fifteen Elder Guardians to lift the door. Luckily, I brought some dynamite! We can easily blast through the mossy stone doors. After the strength test, there is an intelligence test. We will deactivate traps, pick iron locks, solve puzzles, and defeat the boss to get the real deal. There will be gold, food, magical items, and a mysterious potion. Many people have died drinking the potion, as the potion may be anything. From a luck potion to a potion of lightning (which instantly kills you), there are endless possibilities. We're going to need a luck potion if we want to get the cure for that wound."

And so they began their journey. Thirty minutes later, they reached a temple. *Phew!* There was no Guardian here. *BOOM! BOOM!* They blasted into the basement. One big shot from John's rifle quickly killed the Elder Guardian, which happened to be an iron giant. The giant dropped some huge bullets, which was ammunition for John's rifle. They approached a shiny, slick-looking golden chest. Inside were several bandages, an elemental shard which could be used to cast spells related to that element (in this case, rock), a frag grenade, and a mysterious brew.

"Looks like a poison potion. However, we should try it. I have an antidote to any negative potion effect." Frank said. *Slurrpp.* John jumped after he drank the potion. It was a jump potion. He jumped ten feet high!

After they'd explored three more, they were at the final structure. John had found four elemental shards and a sword handle from the ruin chests, so he made a new sword from them. This sword was a sword of gods, as it dealt fire damage, AoE (area of effect) earthquakes, AoE ice traps, AoE waves, and AoE lava tornados. It also did a ton of damage that varied depending on the monster. Right after they went in, they were immediately confronted by five master guardians. A lava tornado quickly took care of that, along with a few swings from John's sword. The next chamber held twelve chests, three on each wall. There was also a special guest: a ten headed dragon. John's sword landed a critical hit, dealing double damage for a total of enough damage that killed the dragon. Along with that, John cut off nine heads. Frank's rifle took care of that last head. The next room was the start of a labyrinth. If they could reach the end of the labyrinth, they could move on. Frank tried to blast through a wall, John shot his rifle at the wall, but the only thing that happened was John's ears ringing from the shot. He switched over to trying to slice it with his sword. Nothing happened.

"Looks like we'll have to blind run our way through." Frank moaned. Thirty seconds in, Frank was looting a goblin and John was clearing out a long passage. As John fired, the sound of a metallic *clink* filled the air as a hot bullet shell hit the floor. By the time John had fired the entire 5 bullets of the rifle's small load, there were five goblins on the ground. There were splotches of dark red that John did not want to think about, red stained leather armor that had been ripped to shreds, swords, spears, helmets splattered with more red, all stuck in the ground and some little sacks with gold drakkens spilling out, as John's bullets had shot them off of their now-dead owners. Frank waved a curved blade that he picked up. Frank then realized that it was way past dinnertime, so he gave his mom a call.

As luck had it, Frank turned around a corner and nearly got stabbed by a skeleton wearing fancy gold armor and held a golden sword. Frank slashed at the skeleton's armor, and the sword sliced through the armor like it was nothing more than soft bread. John found a pack of grenades. He flung one over a wall, and heard sounds that disturbed him. A shard of a sword came flying overhead and came 1 millimeter from hitting John. John suddenly had a great idea. He flung nine (there were a hundred so it didn't really matter.) plasma grenades over the same wall. Then the most unbelievable thing happened. The wall broke, and John and Frank raced through to the other side.

The moment they stepped through the hole, they saw the amazing amount of damage the grenades did. The walls were covered with holes. Round another corner, John met with a robed figure. He introduced himself in a hissing voice that trailed off every minute but John could still hear it. His name was, of course, the Grim Reaper's son.

John pulled out his rifle and Frank pulled out his sword. The Grim Reaper's son twirled his weapon, leaving trails of dust in the air. A deadly hush fell over the dungeon as both sides readied themselves for the long-fought battle ahead. Suddenly, the Grim Reaper's son launched a deadly attack on Frank. John realized that his rifle wouldn't do any good, so he pulled out his own blade. Frank jumped one millisecond too late. With sudden anger, Frank drove his own blade deep into the heart of the Grim Reaper's son. As the Grim Reaper's son clutched the bloodied wound in great agony, John's sword came flying through the air and cut off the fiend's arms. John quickly ran out of the death maze and sat down to rest.

Chapter 11

John felt his throat getting sore, and his stomach was grumbling so loud that he could hear it. He took out his last piece of smoked ham, and munched slowly down on it. He drank the last few drops of water from his canteen, and he felt life temporarily come back to his throat. He munched on the smoked ham, thinking to himself, *I'm gonna have to kill Riley for food now, right? If I don't find food soon, that needs to be done, but i don't want to kill my idiotic dog...* as his thought trailed off, he wondered what he was going to do. John sighed as he thought about the current situation and thought about his grandmother.

"My little dear John, if you are ever lost, don't you worry. There are tushrooms in every little crevice of every planet, so if you look carefully enough, pick some and eat them raw. They have a delicious flavor, like honey bread, so it will be a pleasure to eat!" as John thought about his grandma's words, he also thought about how he was ever going to find the tiniest crevice. John looked at his surroundings. Nothing. Just the typical dry desert. One lonely and dry tree. Millions upon million grains of sand. No sight of a sweet little bulb. Suddenly, he spotted a basket. Inside was a bowl, and several tushrooms. Tushrooms flew into John's mouth as he devoured them one by one. The bulbous shrooms were indeed very sweet like honey bread.

"Oh, and John, remember that you can make tushroom juice that will quench even the thirstiest people." As John thought about this, he squeezed some tushrooms tightly into a bowl in the basket, and soon the bowl was full of golden tushroom nectar. John invited Riley over and she lapped it up with joy.

"Riley, go find some more tushrooms for us, then you can have more of that golden nectar!" John said enthusiastically. Riley yapped her agreement, then wandered off. Five minutes later, the unmistakable noise of Riley's yapping came. John rushed over with the basket, and found seven tushrooms growing on a rock. John put them in his basket, then kept looking. He went into a small cave. There, he found a large group of glowing tushrooms. John knew that these were the cave type. He picked all 23 of them, and went back to his starting point where he had found the basket.

John ate 20 of the tushrooms in the basket, and made ten into delicious tushroom nectar for Riley. Riley lapped up the nectar joyfully, her snout glistening golden in the early morning sunrise. But then, he saw a pack of red-eyed wolves. They were trying to steal the tushrooms! John pulled out his sword and gun. Smoke filled the air as bullet shell after bullet shell hit the ground, all coming from John's gun. John set down his gun and reached for his sword. The air whistled as John swung his sword over and over, cutting off three wolves' legs in one mighty swing.

With all the wolves defeated, John turned back to the tushrooms. He was quite full, and lay down on the warm sand to take a short nap. Riley threw a blanket down just in time to avoid her owner getting covered by sand.

But then, one of the wolves came back and bit John. John pulled out his gun, and shot the wolf right in the chest, giving it a giant bullet hole. The wolf had tushrooms in its mouth, so John took those and ate them. John reloaded his gun, then lay down again. The other wolves launched at John, who shot all of them. More tushrooms were eaten by John, when he heard the annoyed snort of Riley. He had forgotten to give Riley some nectar, so Riley pushed John, then ate the tushrooms herself. John sighed, then went back to sleep. The next morning, John awoke to Riley bottle flipping and landing bottles on John's chest. Riley was flipping her 396th bottle, capping it right on top of the 395th one. John's eyes nearly popped out of his sockets at the sight of so many bottles, all full of water.

"Riley, where did you get these bottles?" asked John. Riley yapped, and here's what she seemed to said:

"I traded your pants, shirt, socks, hat, all the wolf skin, all the wolf meat, and some tushrooms for 400 bottles of electrolyte water, which gives you energy and quenches your thirst at the same time!" John looked down at himself, and sure enough, he only had his white underwear with pink hearts on it.

"RILEY!" John shrieked. Riley just shot John a smug look. John got up, and all of the 396 bottles on his body all fell off, bounced on the sand, then all capped on Riley's back. John fainted from shock. When John awoke, he found some more tushrooms, all inside the basket. John and Riley had another tushroom feast.

John dozed off with an awful lot of tushrooms in his belly, his mind wandering off to replay his stunning victory. As John fell asleep, he could see a dark shadow move across his body as he went into subconsciousness.

John woke up, and realized that the shadow was Riley. Riley was holding up a huge basket of tushrooms, wagging her tail as if she had just saved the world- twice. John rolled his eyes, and Riley peed on John.

"RILEY!" John shrieked. Riley just yapped innocently and gave John her cute sad puppy eyes face. John stared angrily down as Riley trotted around, seeming very self-satisfied. John quickly set to work cleaning himself, while Riley quickly set to work trying to stuff ten tushrooms in her mouth at once. When John was done cleaning himself, Riley had managed to stuff 13 tushrooms into her mouth. John's eyes nearly fell out of their sockets at the sight. There was one more tiny tushroom in the basket, and Riley yapped as if to say, "go ahead, eat it." John angrily stormed over and ate it.

Apparently Riley had peed on that one, too! John vomited the second the tushroom hit his tongue. John tried to spank Riley, but instead got a hand smeared with greenish-brown poop. John's eyes turned red and steam poured from his ears. He flung the poop at Riley, who had swung her tail and easily deflected it onto John's and again. John found a small grenade buried in the sand, and smeared it with poop. The grenade was a Popper, dealing no real damage, just flinging paper (or in this case, poop) everywhere. John pulled the pin, and threw it straight at Riley. The golden doodle used its lightning reflexes to bat the grenade back at John just in time. *BANG!* The bomb went off, exploding poop shrapnel everywhere. John passed out from the bomb and impact.

John wandered around in the desert, and after hours of walking, John found a village. The snakes there were looking for a new king, and immediately approached John with interest.

Chapter 12

General thoughts: John is the snake king and is having a great time commanding the snakes. John also finds the long lost orb of snakes and as soon as he touches it, he gets extremely hard scales.

John felt his breath panting and heard, "You have won the fight. My people, please listen, for this is your new king. You will do what he says, or else I will bestow a curse upon you from the Heathens." John brushed his hand across his forehead which was engulfed in sweat. John heard himself panting deep like John had just ran all the way to the sun and back. John leaned forward a bit, letting more cool air blow on John's back. All the snakes were looking up at him in different expressions John couldn't express. Anger? Happiness? Sadness? John didn't know.

John felt mixed emotions about being the king of the snakes. The sun burned hot on John's face. Lucky sun, it never had to worry about sandstorms or its dog. It just rotated everyday, doing its daily job. John wished he had that life. At least John wasn't lonely. John had friends that supported him. And now, he had these loyal snake companions to guide him.

John felt grateful for at least some support after weeks of being in the dry, eroded planet alone. These giant pythons supported him, loved him, but would they still do all they do if they knew John wasn't a snake? John was a very distant cousin of snakes… after all he had scales didn't he? John wasn't sure they would make an exception for him. John almost certainly knew it.

John had seemed to have taken too much time thinking his thoughts. Everyone had been so silent. Suddenly, a small snake broke the silence. "Speak up you old lazy doofus! We ain't coming here for nothing dingus!" "Yeah! You lazy old doofus probably don't know what you're talking about!" another snake replied. John quickly thought of a speech through his head. John was frantic and he knew his speech was terrible.

"Snakies and Snakelmen,

Though yet of King Philips, our dear king's death

The memory is green and that it us befitted

He roams through thou gates of life

The great king has died

To bear our hearts in grief, and our whole kingdom

To be contracted in one brow of woe

Yet so far hath discretion fought with nature

That we with wisest sorrow think on him"

John finished his speech as his voice trailed off. His speech was followed by a series of applause.

"That was confusing but very prophetic!" a snake yelled.

"Yeah!" a deep gunt added.

John felt proud of himself for coming up with a 5 second speech that took half a second to make. John felt that this was truly an accomplishment.

John walked off the stage as the crowd continued to cheer.

"Snake King! Snake King!" the crowd cheered. John felt sweat starting to form on his forehead for some reason. John walked off behind the stage. He whispered to the stage director, "Where do I go?"

"To the castle. It's right behind us." the stage director replied in a low hiss.

"Thanks." John whispered back. The stage director nodded. John walked to the castle.

The castle was hard to ignore. It looked ghostly, mainly because it was red and gray. It looked like someone hadn't been in it for a long time. Giant webs covered the castle and the castle glowed a purplish color in the sunlight. The castle gave John goosebumps. It's high towers and pointed statues did nothing but scare John. It was like someone had painted a castle from a horror movie and placed it smack in the middle of nowhere.

John didn't want to go anywhere near the castle. In fact, he didn't want to see the castle. The castle looked… undead. The previous king must not have entered the castle. Or the king before that. John was losing count. All John knew was not to enter it.

Although John didn't think that was an option.

John just had this *feeling* that he had to go inside. He didn't know why, how, what, who, or when. He just had this feeling that he would have to go in at some point. He just *knew*. John felt terrified at that prospect.

"All hail the snake king! Master of the Orb!" The crowd cheered. However, John's heart was filled with nervousness, hoping that the snakes wouldn't eat their human king.

Chapter 13

As John was crowned by snakes dressed in velvet and jewels, his mind was full of foreboding. He had nightmares that he would be eaten by other snakes, but he had to admit, it was really cozy in the royal chambers. Every day, servants would serve him hot chocolate and cookies, a wonderful mix. His bed was made out of the fluffiest sheep wool, and the blanket was a thick layer of snake scales. Servants with giant halberds and longswords guarded the entrance to the chambers. John himself was given a longsword with rubies, sapphires, and diamonds encrusted in the handle and blade.

John was kept safe from any danger, but he still suspected that one of the guards would betray him. After all, he *was* the Master of the Orb. John learned that the Orb had mysterious psychokinetic energy that was unbelievably powerful— ten times more powerful than a nuclear bomb.

Then, all the foreboding came true: One of the guards tried stealing the Orb in the night. This was when John learned how very powerful this solid glass ball truly was.

The ball glowed a deep red, gave off an ear-piercing shriek, and burnt the guard's hand. John got up and killed the guard with his longsword. The ball shot a red laser at the body of the snake, and it disintegrated. John was never so stressful in his entire life. He started sweating, having nightmares, and even thinking about running away. John kept his longsword beside him at all times, and started keeping loaded rifles and machine guns nearby. The Orb was like a living companion to John, and he learned that it liked a nice meal of snake sin. The skin would be placed in a bowl and the Orb would use its telepathic powers to grab and eat them. John always liked watching the orb.

One day, the Orb rolled onto the floor and started pulling John. John thought the Orb wanted to go for a walk/roll, so he tagged along. Along the way, the Orb seemed attracted to something in the grass, and it was actually a dead body of a snake.

"Great, so now there are assassins and betraying guards on the loose!" John said, cursing under his breath. The Orb glowed a bright red and John immediately remembered the power of his companion.

That night, John found what looked like a thousand-year-old script in the royal libraries.

A thousand kings our future holds,
But we must not forget our ancestors.
That is why I, King Serpent VII, have forged The Orb.
The Orb shall hold all memories of ancestors,
Along with the power of one billion armies.
If on the winter solstice there is a full moon,
Then your fellow kings will join you.

John knew that tomorrow was the winter solstice, and yesterday he saw a waxing gibbous moon, so tomorrow was bound to be a full moon!

As John waited for midnight to approach, the Orb glowed bright green, and hundreds of snakes appeared from the glow. One of them slid to John's side and whispered in a voice that sounded like the wind,

"*There will be a major invasion at dawn soon.*"

"When is 'soon'?"

"*All signs suggest no more than one wave of the silver moon.*"

"Oh."

As John collected all of the snakes together, he announced that there would be a major invasion in one month at dawn. All of the snakes immediately volunteered to become a soldier and fight for John. Blacksmiths made weapons, carpenters made artillery, engineers sat around and drank coffee while watching the carpenters (and yes, snakes like coffee), a cricket chirped, and someone complained about accidentally smashing his tail with a two-by-four wood piece.

At last, everything was ready. All snakes had a full set of armor and two weapons. Suddenly, a horn sounded, and the invasion started.

Hundreds of monsters stormed into view from the desert haze, but John had five layers of defence. The first was a big wall. Next, there was a moat filled with lava. Then, the invaders would have to cross a cactus field. Once they got through, they would be met by the blades of the snakes' weapons. In the case that they broke through, John and his Orb would be waiting to blast them into atoms. The invaders' axes and sledgehammers easily broke the wall, but when it crumbled, it took some soldiers out as well. The lava was a disaster for the invaders. The general rushed forward and stopped right at the edge of the moat, but got bumped by thirty or so soldiers who also fell in. Swords of the invaders cut the cactus like a farmer's sickle cutting wheat. Within a minute, all the cactus was cut down. A volley of arrows soared through the air and mowed down the front row of attackers like they were nothing. Then, catapults and trebuchets were launched into the crowd, knocking down and smushing about 50 invaders. Many more were utterly destroyed as 3,578 snakes charged in with swords ready. John and his Orb picked off the remaining enemies one by one, until the entire battlefield was just dead monsters and the occasional dead snake.

That night, John and the snakes held a huge banquet in the Snake King's honor. Bakers baked lumpy muffins that looked like blobs, The Orb was given a bowl of purple and silver mush, everyone feasted on roast turkey and drank cactus juice by the gallons, and musicians played instruments with their tails. John held a shooting competition afterwards, and each contestant lined up with a big rifle, and bullets whizzed through the air as every snake and John shot their guns at a target. John was the winner, and got to keep the gun he used. John gave the second place winner his longsword, and the third place winner got a solid hunk of gold. Then the feasting and activities continued. There was Fruit Ninja, another shooting competition, a wine-drinking competition, and even a farting competition. For the farting competition, the contestants were given refried beans and a gas mask.

The Orb used its psychokinetic powers to fire a pistol at a wine bottle, and the wine exploded out of the bottle and into the crowd. Everyone opened their mouths and got at least one drop of the purple grape wine. John brought out an exquisite gun with a silver finish and a 37-karat gold barrel. The mahogany was polished, and the sight, which is used to aim, was made of pure platinum! John fired once, and a bullet came soaring out and embedded itself into a replica of a deer head. The crowd roared its approval, and John fired another bullet into the deer. The deer slumped over and the crowd gave John a standing ovation.

"Would anyone else like to try out this beauty?" John asked. Everyone quickly raised their tails and hissed in agreement.

John was nearly deafened by the roar of all the snakes, but picked a young blacksmith to shoot the gun. No matter how hard the blacksmith tried, John was indubitably a better shot.

John then brought out the grand finale of the banquet. A knife thrower and a lady stepped on stage. The knife thrower was blindfolded, and threw a knife at the lady snake. But instead of narrowly missing, the knife thrower cackled evilly and killed the snake! John unmasked the knife thrower to reveal Ophelia! John grabbed his fancy gun and shot three rounds into Ophelia's arm.

"That was a warning shot. Next time it's the head." John warned. Ophelia ducked behind one of the tables and John ran behind another table. The snakes fled to the outer parts of the banquet and watched while chanting, "GO John" over and over again. Ophelia threw a grenade, but the seller had given her a dud, and it failed to explode. John threw a grenade at Ophelia's hiding place, and a shower of shrapnel drove into Ophelia's flesh, knocking her down.. Fifteen bullets slammed into a torch near Ophelia, making it explode into a fiery frenzy. Ophelia managed to dodge most of the burning splinters, but was badly hurt when John fired ten more shots into her leg. She slipped on a twig, and sprained her ankle. John walked up with an axe, raising it to Ophelia's neck.

"If I ever see you again, you're dead."

And with that, Ophelia was escorted out of the kingdom by guards, and John could still hear cursing even when Ophelia was gone. John lowered his rifle, and the celebration continued with broken tables and bloodstained chairs. The wine bottles were smashed and the food was covered with sand, so new food and wine was brought out. Just then, a group of masked snakes came out from the crowd and knocked John out. The last thing he saw was a bag tied around him.

John awoke with a start. His butt hurt, and he was lying in the sand. Suddenly, he jerked upright. He was no longer in the kingdom of snakes!

Chapter 14

John felt ashamed but grateful at the same time. At least the snakes hadn't killed John. John shuddered at the thought. He practiced his 50-Headed alpha moon wolf spell. Glowing swirls danced across John's palm. Gradually, it turned into a regal and broad wolf with 50 heads. John tried making the wolf slash with its paws. The wolf simply disappeared. John sighed.

Suddenly, John felt a jolt of abrupt panic. All of John's supply were left in the kingdom of 射栿福! John couldn't just go back… he might be attacked. . . John panicked. What would he do? How would he do? Why would he do that? When would he do it? Where would he do? All his supplies were gone. It was impossible to get them back. The snakes would never allow him to go back. They said it themself.

He began fruitlessly scavenging for items. Occasionally, there would be skeletons on the ground with an empty rifle or pistol, but no useful items. John came across several oases and some coconut trees.

After several hours of random wandering, John found the ruins of a village. He began tearing through closets, dumping out chest contents, and searching every part of the houses. One of the blacksmith chests had a sword with a diamond blade, some chipped hammers, and some scrap iron. John took the sword, and kept looking.

He found a rifle that looked like it was new, some bullets, and a full suit of leather armor. John struggled with the tunic and leggings, but managed to get them on. He found three grenades in an armorsmith shop. He also found some shotgun shells, scattered across the floor. John picked them up, and set them back down. He found five rifle bullet shells, a few splotches of blood, and hidden in a corner was a corpse. It had a pistol clutched in one hand, and a grenade in the other.

John searched through other houses, and found more corpses, each carrying some useless weapon, and their flesh rotting away. Some had axes embedded in their chests, some had arrows, some had a red skull from caked blood from bullet wounds. One of the corpses, the mayor, wore a tattered bright red cape that was splattered dark red with blood, 17 arrows piercing through her stomach. John guessed that this was a massacre. But then, John saw a goblin carrying a crossbow sprawled out on the floor, eyes unblinking.

"Goblin raid," John muttered. Several other goblins lay dead, some without a few body parts. John suddenly heard a goblin squeal, and whirled around to find three goblins, all in iron armor, one wielding a sword, another holding two axes, and the leader carrying a crossbow. John grabbed a battered shield from one of the fallen villagers, and turned back at the goblins. Arrows, axes, and knives whizzed through the air, all embedding themselves in John's shield with a *thunk!* John threw a grenade, killing all three goblins. As they writhed in pain, John walked over with his diamond sword. The blade scraped against the messy cobblestone floor, making an ominous scratching sound. He struck out at one of the goblins, spraying blood in a wide arc, "following" the blade for several seconds.

Big mistake. John saw an approaching swarm of goblins, all carrying axes, knives, grenades, or crossbows. John snatched up a pistol and fired at one of the grenade goblins. The bullet struck the grenade, and it detonated. A wide circle was made where the bomb had exploded, killing all goblins in the blast radius. John kept on firing with the pistol, occasionally stopping to block or swipe at the goblins with his sword. An axe flew through the air and thunked onto John's shield. The shield, unable to withstand too much force, shattered.

John grabbed the throwing knives of the shield's splinters and flung them into the wave of goblins. The front line quickly fell, each goblin clutching their wounds as they toppled over. John threw his last two canisters, and they exploded in a burst of green acid. Goblins did everything they could to get out of the way, but many were still caught in the blast. John grabbed a machine gun from a fallen villager and started firing. Goblins fell left and right, and John fired more bullets. The ground started to take on a reddish color as each goblin fell, squealing. The gun had a bayonet attached to it, so John threw the bayonet at one of the goblins. The bayonet sunk into the goblin's chest, piercing its puny leather armor and into its flesh. John threw down the gun and charged, sword extended like a spike. He impaled three goblins, slid the sword out of their green bodies, and backflipped away. One of the goblins was carrying a rifle. John killed the goblin, then took the rifle. Bullets flew through the angry mob as the rifle fired away. Bullet shells bounced around on the cobblestone ground as John fired. Goblins took out shields, but the onslaught of bullets easily tore through the wooden shields. The rifle had run out of ammo, so John charged in once again. The diamond blade made large swaths of destruction, sunlight glinting off of its blood-stained tip. Goblins fell like chopped grass, iron armor shredded and multiple slash wounds across the chest. John fought with a fury that he had never seen inside him before, driving his sword through multiple goblins at a time. John killed goblin after goblin, their bloodstained weapons dropping to the ground. John picked up a rifle from a fallen goblin and fired into the swarm. An unfortunate goblin was struck in the head by the bullet, clutching its wound as it doubled over. This gave John an idea. He swung the rifle through the ranks of the goblins, knocking several down. The goblins toppled on top of each other, forming a giant domino reaction. John fired blindly into the heap of goblins, knowing that he would hit one. He charged in with his sword, slashing downwards. After he had made it through the first two yards of goblins, The diamond sword looked more like a ruby sword. He continued to strike the goblins on the ground, bringing death and destruction wherever the blade was. He threw a grenade into the gory mess, and a red ball erupted out of the swarm. Goblin guts and weapon splinters showered John and the village. John barfed as he batted away a bloody arm. The remaining goblins scrambled to their feet and zipped away, but John's rifle picked them off one by one.

John looked around at the bloodied scene, and then down at his body. There were more than 100 projectiles, yet he felt no pain whatsoever. There were at least a hundred goblin bodies. All of them had at least 70% of their bodies covered with blood. Their torsos, legs, and heads were covered with slashes, bullet holes, or stab wounds. John rummaged through the corpses, and found several useless items. Yet one seemed to stand out: a red dagger glowing purple with enchants. John pulled up statistics, and the dagger had an enchantment that returns it to you once you throw it. It deals 25-150000 damage depending on the level of the enemy, and can sometimes pierce multiple enemies. John saw a goblin peeking around a corner, and threw the dagger. The dagger flew through the air, impaled the goblin, and flew back to John. John saw that the dagger also had a poison coating. He threw the dagger at another peeking goblin, and this time it took the goblin's head right off! John caught the dagger mid-air, and walked away from the ruins.

On the way out, John faced two heavily armored goblins, both carrying halberds and wearing armor. John threw the dagger, but one of the guards caught it and pocketed it! John pulled out his rifle, and ended the guards' lives right then and there. John walked nonchalantly past the guards' bodies and out of the ruins.

John had seen an overwhelming amount of fighting that day, so he lay down in the warm sun and took a nice long nap.

Chapter 15

John considered and considered. The snake tribe had taken his items, but they did leave him with his diamond sword. He chopped at a moose skull, or at least it looked like a moose skull. It was actually a Wendigo, a towering moose-like carnivore that feasted on human flesh and wore a moose skull. The Wendigo rose from the sand and charged at a pack of ferocious tigers. With a single headbutt, the Wendigo's sharp antlers impaled two tigers, and seriously wounded three more. John stared in horror and awe. He quickly backed away from the battle, not wanting to be the next one sent to the Heathens.

Fortunately, the Wendigo saw some cactus and thought it was a very nice toy. It began violently shredding the cactus, unaware of the many thorns. John threw the Wendigo some steak, and it turned to John. The Wendigo smiled, and ate the steak. John breathed a sigh of relief, knowing that he had befriended the Wendigo, at least for now.

The Wendigo came off to be very helpful! It helped John through tricky situations, but then, there was a blood-curdling shriek. A mythical creature known as a Manananggal flew by, holding a dangerous-looking scimitar, a large curved knife. John and the Wendigo attacked the Manananggal, but it flew up out of their reach. John reached for his self-defense gun that he carried around, but he only felt a rifle. John fired the rifle, and a big bullet streaked toward the Manananggal. The giant shot was easily deflected by the glowing scimitar of the flying horror, so the Wendigo jumped incredibly high and impaled the Manananggle in its upper torso. As it came down, the Wendigo ripped the Manananggle's heart loose and happily ate it. John picked up the scimitar, and studied it. He swung it at his Longsword, and it cut through the bejeweled blade like it was hot butter. John immediately kept the scimitar, and turned around to see the Wendigo picking at some of the Manananggle's rib bones.

John got to test out the scimitar immediately after, because a troll appeared in full reinforced titanium armor, complete with a titanium sword. One strike from the scimitar cut the troll's legs clean off. Another slash, and the troll was slumped over.

John got the titanium armor that was undamaged, the Wendigo got the meat, and they walked off. Another Sand Wyrm, a small army of trolls, and a Sand Golem later, John had so much gory stuff that will not be named on his sword that the metal looked like it was painted red. The Wendigo burped, having eaten that much flesh. John had acquired another rifle. John found a zombie town, a place where zombies live. The rifle tore through the first 37 zombies, but took a few more bullets to break armor. Zombies rushed in from all directions, carrying axes, hoes, bows, auto-pistols, the occasional chainsaw, flamethrowers, and so on. Bullets whizzed through the air, embedding themselves into zombies, armor, the ground, and trees.

At one point, someone threw an axe. The axe flew toward John, who neatly cut it into shards and splinters. More bullets, more dead zombies, and more dropped weapons.

Fifteen minutes later, all the zombies lay dead. The Wendigo didn't know where to start, to it this was a fancy banquet with hundreds of delicacies. However, the Wendigo took one sniff at the rotten meat, then immediately turned away, shaking its head.

As John munched on the food and walked along, an eccentric zombie wearing tattered clothes and an underwear on his ear tugged at John's leg and whispered,

"I predict that you shall rise up and survive this planet,
and it can't get worse, can it?

Bloody battles, horrific monsters, and deadly traps,

But your journey ends soon, with just three claps.

You're brave and fearless, but death is inevitabl…"

The zombie fell limp, and the red light in his eyes faded into darkness as the zombie died.

"To the well-organized mind, death is but the next great adventure. Rest in peace, zombie. Or should I say, rot in peace." as the dead zombie slumped over, rain started falling, fitting the mood perfectly. John stared in silence, unable to speak. Even though it was a zombie, John didn't want anyone dying unless it was a battle. He picked some flowers, put them in the zombie's lap, and quietly walked away.

Since the zombie town was in a forest, John collected some fruit and headed away from the town, the Wendigo following close behind. Right outside the town, He found an Ashunta army waiting for him. A messenger gave him a note that read,

Regarding the killing of the Ashunta general, Korimha DeVamug, we have come to avenge his death. Please, come with us or fight us.

"I will fight you right here," John said. As he opened fire, one thousand Ashunta troops marched forward with spears raised. The Wendigo charged in and impaled six Ashunta warriors in one swing. John charged forward, carving great swaths of destruction where the glowing blade went. Ashunta warrior weapons, armor, and bodies went flying as the Wendigo headbutted the angry mob. John's rifle ripped through the leather tunics of the front line, but had a hard time clearing out the more heavily armed Ashuntas. Suddenly, a mage wearing crimson robes strode out and cast a spell. A volley of magical missiles streaked through the air and exploded all around John, tearing apart the desert sand and making huge craters. John threw a grenade, and it exploded into tiny bits of shrapnel. The shrapnel punched through leather and chain armor, but it only dented the iron armor. John kept firing the rifle, the bullet shells ejecting and flying into the sand. Ashuntas fell, one by one, the rifle dropping warriors left and right. The mage cast another spell, this time sending a wave of compressed air at John, but John leapt out of the way just in time, dragging the Wendigo along. John sent a wave of bullets, killing the mage. Ashunta warriors charged again, this time fatally wounding the Wendigo. But, the Wendigo's acidic blood boiled all the charging warriors, melting their armor and shriveling their bodies like raisins.

After the fighting, the Wendigo staggered, let out a final shriek, then fell to the ground, blood dripping and pooling in the sand. John charged at the remaining Ashuntas, seething with rage. The sword glowed bright red, seeming to reflect John's anger. In a flash of red, John drove the blade through the ranks of warriors, until there was only the general left. John killed the horse, and was ready to kill the general, when another mage appeared.

"Wait, before you take your revenge, I can revive the Wendigo." John reluctantly agreed, and the mage healed the Wendigo. The general wet his pants and fled, still assuming that John was going to kill him. The mage also made a little puddle and fled the second he revived the Wendigo. John just smiled and walked away, eager to get away from the wet spots. He arrived at a deserted inn, but the bar still had lots of beer, wine, and food in it. John and the Wendigo ate like pigs, trashed the bar, and left. A moment later, they came rushing back in as Siren Head nearly ate John. Three slashes and a bag of rice later, The Wendigo found out how to make a new delicacy: the Siren Head Sushi. It gobbled down the giant sushi, and they left again.

John met some cactus monsters, monsters made of cacti. John's rifle easily punched neat holes through each of them. Until John ran out of bullets.

John panicked as he realized that he was running out of bullets.

The bullets went out into the darkness of night as the sun set. John found a big branch, took out a lighter, and made a torch. He found a chest full of dynamite and one backpack, and took it. Now that he had 50 pieces of dynamite stuffed into his backpack, life was much more stressful. If a stray bullet were to hit him, it was all over.

Just then, the Wendigo turned on John. Or something behind him.

Chapter 16

John felt terror rise in his throat. The beast crawled closer. As it came closer John saw his fate. The wendigo took no notice. It was busy attacking a broad shouldered tiger. The tiger growled viciously but it was no match for the wendigo. The tiger slowly, gracefully, fell to the ground with a soft *thump*, a nameless, faceless creature. Nobody knew and nobody cared.

The creature behind the Wendigo slaughtered the Wendigo silently, under cover of darkness. The creature had slashed Wendigo's throat and what was left there was a thin line of dark red. Blood began gushing out furiously and Wendigo's eyes started going blank. The thin line of red began to grow to a giant black scar. John pitied the Wendigo but that made one less danger to him. The creature that had killed the forest monster scurried behind giant trees. John may have lost a powerful enemy but he had gained a more powerful enemy.

John finally noticed that night had fallen and the stars were glowing. The moon however, was a deep red as if stained by the pool of blood by the dead Wendigo. John didn't want to sleep next to the dead wendigo but truthfully, he didn't want to sleep anywhere near the creature who had killed the Wendigo. John knew he had to sleep but he knew he didn't want to sleep. That creature might kill him. If he killed John tonight then what was the point of even trying to survive. John cursed under his breath, allowing the tiniest of sounds. It was nearly impossible for any living creature to hear it—or at least any kind of alien that might possibly be a distant relative to those long lost "Human" creatures.

Apparently, the humans had discovered some aliens on the "red planet". Five sneaky humans had fallen in love with the aliens and the human race had died out. Only the aliens and their hybrids existed but then the actual aliens died out from old age. Now many of the distant human relatives were either Jokulan or Casoli but there the mixed offspring.

John was thinking about that memory as he fell asleep. John didn't realize the unfamiliar steps walking outside John's little bubble of thoughts. He didn't realize the giant black face that loomed over John. When John finally looked up again, he realized that there was something above his head. Something with a shiny black face and black tophat. The creature, Babadook, had arrived.

John knew there was nothing he could do. The Babadook represented ultimate grief and loss. If John tried anything too dangerous, The Babadook could do something terrible to him…. Or his family and friends.

John found a familiar weapon - his sword! Right next to it, there was his rifle! John eagerly picked up the weapons, feeling a course of energy as he held the blade up. The Babadook pulled out a wicked-looking sword, and thus began the longest duel in dueling history.

In the first nine hours, John and the Babadook were merely exchanging blows, holding small truces to eat, then continuing to fight. But then, John summoned a very big lava tornado and burnt half of the Babadook to a crisp. The Babadook only grinned its eerie grin, and stabbed John in the arm. John then thrusted his own blade into the Babadook's chest, and the Babadook lay crumpled on the ground. John bandaged his own arm, then pulled his sword out from the Babadook's chest. Blood dripped down from both combatant's wounds as John pulled out more gauze. The Babadook still lay motionless, although John could still hear faint breathing. The Babadook suddenly got up, its burnt half crumbling into dust. He pulled out two emerald daggers, and the second round of the longest duel in dueling history began.

The emerald blades summoned an emerald maelstrom that whirled around the Babadook. John's sword summoned a magma tornado around John. Emerald met magma as the two storms clashed, opening in the middle to make an emerald/magma barrier. At one point, John shot the Babadook, and the emerald storm disappeared as the Babadook crumpled to the ground once again. This time John couldn't hear breathing anymore. The Babadooks weapons, the emerald blades and the dark iron rapier, lay next to the dead Babadook. John cleaned his own sword, then headed away.

After several hours of walking, the sun was setting. John found a lost city. The moment he stepped foot into the lost city, he was greeted by unwelcoming Fallen Warriors. The Fallen Warriors were warriors, long dead since the Cataclysm that created the Universes. They carried ancient weapons which have long since been forgotten, and wore the earliest version of armor, with ancient runes encrypted inside the metal plating. Facing one was a real danger, and killing one would bring you great fortune when selling the armor and weapon. John noticed that they had huge biceps, they were ten feet tall, and that they both carried giant swords. Suddenly, he felt a sharp pain in his neck. The last thing he saw was another Fallen Warrior picking him up.

John awoke in a room, strapped to a plank of wood. Fortunately, he could see his weapons on a table nearby. Unfortunately, he could also see a heck ton of warriors watching him with great interest. In an instant, John reached into his pocket and pulled out a large knife and cut himself free of the ropes. He drove the knife into the Fallen Warriors one by one, then grabbed his sword and ran.

John held his sword, running through the streets of the ruins. At one point, he threw his large knife at a Fallen Warrior, and killed him. John raced over and picked up the gear and put it on. The Fallen Warrior had a sword, its blade glistening a greenish hue in the cold morning light. John took a moment to admire the beautiful sight, then continued onward. Another Fallen Warrior came into view as John ran, panting. The warrior carried a curved blade and swung it, seeming intent on cutting John into strips. John's sword streaked through the air to block, and thus another duel began.

Bits of metal flew through the air as a strong hand slammed a curved blade down on John, who reacted just in time. John swung with all his might, but the Warrior's armor was too thick. But then John realized that the warrior's armor was plate mail, meaning that it was a bunch of iron plating stacked on top of each other. John stuck his sword between two pieces of plating, and the Fallen Warrior cried in pain as the sword found flesh. This made the battle easier, since John had solid armor. Soon enough, the Fallen Warrior was slumped over.

Chapter 17

John realized that he had to find a lot of supplies, as he has either lost them or they have broken. The only thing that he had now was a plain rifle with almost no bullets, his clothes, and Riley. He found an axe with a little crack on it in the ground, and it was better than using his fists to fight. Perfectly, another monkey mage appeared, just to make John's day better. John quickly chopped at the monkey with the sandy axe the second his eyes met the piercing eyes of the monkey. The monkey screeched with fury and pain and winced at the pain of the cut on its leg. The monkey lunged at John with anger.

John cried out in surprise as the monkey kicked the axe out of his hand and backflipped away. The mage happily took the axe, glad to have an advantage. John quickly snapped out of his senses and pulled the trigger of his gun, but there was just a plain little *click!* John's gun was empty! He ducked as the monkey swiped at him with the axe. John spotted a weakness and punched the monkey mage right in the belly. The impact was so painful for the monkey that it dropped the axe. His eyes were as wide as olives, his face twisted with pain. In a state of pain and anger, he threw a small rune onto John. The rune slowed John to the speed that would make a snail laugh. John, in a state of slowness, threw a rather large bottle onto the monkey's head. The moment it touched the monkey's head, it cried out in agony. Miraculously, the monkey was a fire mage, and the bottle that John threw on the monkey was none other than a water bottle! The monkey ran away grabbing its poor head.

John blocked its path. The monkey begged for mercy and quickly dispelled the slowness. Then it slowly cast a different spell. A fiery sword began to appear in front of John. The sword was a beautiful burnt orange, with bits of orange clinohumite (which is a gem) and blood red rubies on the handle. The blade was a fine piece of hardened topaz. In the reflection, John could see himself going home.

"The sword is called the Sword of Hope, and whoever looks into the blade will see their greatest dream." the monkey squealed in a high-pitched voice. John let the monkey go and the monkey gave him one last thing: some fruit.

"Why would we need fruit?" asked John.

"It is Firefruit. It protects you from any sort of fire damage for 5 hours after consumption. It is one of the many Elemental Fruits." the monkey explained.

"Do you have anything else, perhaps some food or water?" John asked.

"Not to worry, I have a bunch of food. Let's see… I have half a pound of cheese, five bags of Flavor Bombs (Extra Cheesy), one pack of gum, ten liters of water, a roast turkey, fifteen packs of Jolukasatees, and some sourdough bread crumbs." Mused the monkey as he rummaged through its knapsack.

John took everything but the bread crumbs. He then gave the monkey several drakkens and was thanked generously. John felt a friendship blooming between him and the creature. He decided that after all, a monkey may be useful in his journey. Unfortunately for John, this particular monkey kept its intense gaze on the cheese. John sighed.

Suddenly, the monkey let out an ear-piercing shriek and charged at a bush. John stared blankly at the bush and the monkey. The monkey hurled an enormous fireball at the dry, shriveled shrub. The shrub instantly burst into flames, and out jumped a baby sand golem. Now, even baby golems are really strong. The golem used an attack called "Sandy Death" and threw a gigantic sand clump at John. The monkey formed a magma wall in front of John, and then it hurled the wall at the golem. The golem shattered on impact, and John was awed at the monkey's abilities. John was also amazed by the item that the golem dropped: a small crystal made up of red lasers. John touched it and instantly regretted it, as it hurt a lot. The crystal pulsed once, then dropped into the sand. Seconds later, a wriggling beast known as a Sand Wyrm burst out of the sand, the crystal inside its mouth!

The Wyrm was like a normal worm, except it had rough, scaly skin and a giant mouth that could have swallowed John's entire condo. Green scales lined the wyrm's body and a forked tongue that flicked in and out. Also, it was about ten million times bigger than a normal worm.

The monkey mage summoned dual katanas with the "Conjure Weapon" spell and hurled them both at the Wyrm's mouth. The swords hit the inside of the wyrm's mouth and the Wyrm reared back in pain.

John shot the Wyrm with his gun, killing several flakes of skin. Riley raced around the wyrm and bit down hard and the end of its scaly tail. Its tail flicked and poor Riley flew across sand and landed with a thud. John felt something heating inside him and did something he never would have possibly imagined. John grabbed the hilt of his sword and pulled it out of its sheath. John roared and scrambled up the snakey body of the wyrm.

Once John reached the wyrms head, he drove the sword straight through the top of the Wyrm's head. Blood sprayed all around and on top of John. The wyrm collapsed into a heap and lay still.

Once John was sure the Wyrm had died he raced over to Riley. The crystal popped out from the Wyrm and the monkey caught it with a jar it conjured.

Inside, they could feel the crystal pulsing. John picked up Riley and got this weird idea to place his own gun into the jar and mix it with the crystal. He plopped the rifle into the jar (it surprisingly fit) and they watched as the jar began to glow with light. When the light died, a gun that was glowing with golden energy popped out. The machine gun was now fit for a god, not a mortal being like John.

The gun was remade, now glowing with power, and could shoot three times as far and three times the punch. The gun had a shiny gold polish, and had a longer barrel. It shot explosive rounds that were on fire, or lightning bolts. There was now a switch that you could switch to toggle between the ammo. John instantly tested it out. He didn't have to worry about ammo, because the "Endless Bullets" perk gave him no limits to ammo. When he shot the explosive round at a tree, the tree was instantly reduced to splinters. And when he shot the lightning round at a tree, there was the loudest of bangs, and the tree was completely gone. No atoms, no splinters, none. John was amazed.

Perfectly, another Sand Wyrm crawled out of the sand. This Wyrm was much bigger than the previous one, and this one was covered with sharp spines! First, John tried the explosive round. The explosive round was so powerful, that it killed… a few spines. John stared blankly at the tiny amount of damage. Then he switched to the lightning bolt shot and shot the gun once again at the Sand Wyrm. The lightning blast managed to blow off the Wyrm's tail, but the wyrm still had a lot of its tail. John blasted and blasted, but it had no effect on the Wyrm. Then the Wyrm reared back and opened its mouth, forming a sandy clump in its mouth, but one second before the sandy clump formed, John shot a lightning bullet into the mouth of the creature. The creature reared back even more, this time without a head. John had now found some resources. He was exhausted, and collapsed by a tree, munching on some Flavor Bombs.

"Mmph, geese ore yo wiwicious" John said through a crammed mouthful of the cheesy puffs. What he meant to say was, "mmm, these are so delicious." he gave the monkey a slice of cheese, which it devoured immediately and made a squeaking sound. John did not want to litter, but he had nowhere to throw his bag away. The monkey gave him a trash bag. John thanked the monkey and cut off a leg from the roasted turkey. It was cold, so the monkey breathed fire on it. John ate it, but the moment his lips touched the crispy, tender meat, he instantly passed out because of the pain. When he came to, the monkey was leaning over him, asking him in alien language if he wanted some salt. He didn't know how he understood that, but he somehow managed to do it. John sat up and tried again to eat the turkey leg. This time, the monkey added cheese sauce and salt on it. John's mouth instantly went full rage mode on the leg. He devoured the entire thing in less than two seconds! His mouth was covered with sauce, salt bits, and drool. The monkey gave him a napkin. John wiped his mouth and lay down to sleep. But he kept the cheesy foods under his "pillow" which was actually his backpack.

He woke with much alarm when he heard gunshots, then the loud noise of a rifle firing. John grabbed his own rifle and fired a bullet at where the monkey was shooting. The shot struck a troll carrying a grenade. Meanwhile, John was shooting blindly around him. One shot stuck a goblin, the next stuck another golem. John turned the power knob to max, and flew back ten feet as he fired his next shot, which went through a bear, a goblin, a troll, a golem, and a sand dune. The sand dune did not really care, but all the other targets flew back ten feet. They crashed into the sand dune, and the sand dune didn't really care about that, either. The gun barrel was sizzling from that way-too-overpowered shot. The monkey pulled out dual revolvers from his sack and totally smoked the rest of the assassins. He twirled his revolvers like a western gunslinger before blowing the gun tips. *What a show-off,* John thought.

But it wasn't over, because the sand was wriggling, then *WHOOSH!* The sand fell away to reveal a giant thing with a giant mouth. John couldn't think of anything else to describe it, so it will now be known as "Thing." the monkey, now dressed in an outlaw poncho, fired its dual revolvers at the Thing. The Thing flinched from the meager damage, so John fired a bullet at the Thing. Once the smoke cleared, there was the Thing, standing there as if it had gotten hit by a pillow, not an insanely powerful bullet. The monkey conjured up another rifle and sent out a load of bullets enough to rip a Sand Wyrm to shreds. Yet the Thing just stood there as if he had just gotten a massage, not a barrage of bullets. The gods saw this from the Heathens, and assisted John. The god told John to throw out some cheese. John did as told and threw out a wheel of cheese. The Thing instantly dived for the cheese. John ran away while the Thing was eating.

The monkey ran and John sat on its back. John hovered a piece of cheese in front of the monkey's face, so the monkey ran, thinking that it would catch the cheese. The monkey ran for a while. John was sick and tired of running. Why was he even running? Why couldn't he just grow wings and fly away? Well that was impossible. Even if he did learn to magically fly, he would go too fast and the monkey would fall out of sight very quickly.

After what seemed like a long time, they reached an oasis. The oasis was not very deep, only about three feet, but its water was deep blue, so it looked like 20 feet deep.

"FINALLY, WATER IS HERE!" John exclaimed cheerfully. He ran up to take a humongous gulp and gulped down a lot of sand. Then he filled his water jug, and let the monkey take a sip from the oasis, too. The oasis had three coconut trees near it, or at least they looked like coconuts. John jumped up six inches, then, when he obviously failed, he became angry and kicked the coconut tree so hard that the leaves rattled and five coconuts came falling down, all aimed for John's head. They hit John, and was quite knocked out after that. The sound that woke John from sleep was the monkey trying to open the coconut. John grabbed his sword and sliced the fruit neatly in half. The sound of eating and slurping could be heard by a bug, who wandered by, looking for the source of the sound. It bit John's toe, and then carried the dropped coconut away. John decided to name his monkey. He named it "Blazer," since it had bright orangish-red fur and was a fire mage.

John continued his walk out into the desert, and immediately realized that he didn't have nearly enough water. Uh oh. John's head began to swim, and his vision was getting dark around the corners...

Chapter 19

John was tired and thirsty, the intense heat of the desert was weighing on him. The sun was more than half past the horizon line and John could already hear owls hooting. John needed a rest. A rest sounded nice to him. After all the troubles he had, all John needed was a good night's rest.

John set down his pack and started building up a tent with a pack he had found in the desert. It was dark green and not very interesting. On there, there were some alien words scribbled that John couldn't read but he guesses it said, "Stay Out". At least that is what John would write. He couldn't think of anything else to write.

By the time John had finished setting up the tent the sun had broken past the horizon and little creatures of the night started scuttling out. Riley was already dozing off in the tent. It was a good thing she didn't snore. At least John hoped she didn't. With all the owl screeches and all the chilling rattles, John almost couldn't hear anything.

John snuck into the tent and set down the pillow. He didn't have time to think before his eyelids were closing. John didn't dream. Or at least he thought so until he started dreaming. At first, John thought he saw a purple human. John focused his vision on the thing that was coming for him. It looked like a human to John but as it came closer John quickly realized what it was. It was a purple rotting corpse.

The rotting corpse was treading closer and closer to John by the minute. It walked slowly. It had truly horrifying features. Purple and blue blood were gushing out of the sides and there was no flesh, just rotting skin and bone. There was a giant and nasty cut down the side of its leg and blood trailed off behind it.

Its face was moaning but at the same time, twisted in a cruel smile. Its eyes were missing from its sockets and what was left behind were endless jagged holes.

The corpse continued advancing toward John. Its hand was reaching out, as if it was hoping to grab John and strangle him. "Your kind did thisssss to me….. " Came a horrible and twisted hiss. The corpse advanced on John, "You will join me….." Came another hiss. John looked around frantically. There was nowhere to go. All around John, tall black towers loomed over him. There were skeletons watching on the top. Each skeleton had bright red eyes. John faced the front again. The rotting corpse was next to him and in John's ear, he hissed, "I will come for you….. Last warning…"

John threw himself up and out of his sleep. He could feel sweat rolling down his face. Dawn was just breaking out the horizon. The hooting of owls and hissing of snakes had faded away and what was left were the chirps of the morning birds. The sky was orange and yellow and a bit red at the top. All he needed was a good night's sleep. He didn't get a good night's sleep but what he did get was a beautiful morning. John wanted to start on a good day so he read a quote from his book.

"Everything has beauty but not everyone sees it -Confucious" John read out loud.

John quickly thought about what it meant. It was easy! It meant "Beauty is everywhere!" John grinned. He was ready and pumped for a day of travelling to the west. There was an old myth about the west.

To the west, there are statues. Giant statues. But these statues aren't any statues, they are magical. Each of them has a realm. There are 14 statues. The first one is called Hallola. She is the statue of hope. To enter her realm, you must pay a token which can be found in Hallola's dress that she wears. Then you can enter her realm and all your hopes will come true. To come out of the realm, you must give away a loved one to pay for the hopes you have cherished. The second statue's name is Aife. She is the statue of protection. Everything you want to be protected will be protected once you enter her realm. To enter her realm, you must enter the prayer of Bellona. To exit her realm, your own protection must lower so much that you cannot withstand anything. The third statue's name is Muriel. Muriel is the statue of luck. To enter her realm you must have entered another one of the realms. Inside her realm, you can have all the great luck of anything you do. To exit the realm, you must lose your most important memory. The next statue is Aphrodite. Aphrodite is the statue of love and reincarceration. To enter the realm, you must sing her a song. If she enjoys it, she will let you into her realm. Inside her realm, all the loved ones you ever had will come to you. The loved ones that died will reincarcerate. To exit her realm you must lose a loved one. The next statue is Lyssa. Lyssa is the statue of calmness. To enter her realm, you must offer a book or scroll. Only then, she will let you in. In the realm, you will have the power to manage emotion and calmness. To exit her realm, your calmness will go away. The next statue is Aiden. He is the statue of light. To enter his realm, you must win a chess game against him. If you lose, You will be banished to the realm of Lucifer. When you enter Aiden's realm, you see an amazing future and you get stuck in the moment. Happiness will be all you feel. To exit Aiden't realm, you must let reality come to you. The next statue is Lucifer. Lucifer is the statue of darkness. Lucifer will try to lure you to his realm. If you get in there are horrid punishments awaiting you. They are flaying you alive, whipping you until you die, putting you lost and alone in a forest full of werewolves, turning you over to a hungry monster, and pushing a boulder up a hill for eternity. Lucifer can always come up with cruel ways to tempt you to   come. The next statue is Tivona. Tivona is the statue of Eternity. To enter her realm you must say the oath of truth and you must mean it. In her realm, you will find eternal life. You will live forever, no matter what happens. To exit Tivona's realm you must lose part of your soul. Here is a warning about Tivona: She is brother to Lucifer. Her power is eternal, no matter what emotion you feel. You could be eternally sad or happy. The next statue is Holly. Holly is the statue of Earth. To enter her realm, you must have the knowledge on what lies below earth. In Holly's realm, there are beautiful landscapes with birds chittering happily and deers gracefully moving through the wind. The scenery is very distracting but at the same time, lovely. To exit holly's realm, you must watch horrors of the reality of earth. The Next statue is Lilian. Lilian is the statue of the happy futures. To enter Lilian's realm, you must play a game of Set with Lilian. Of course, if you lose, you get stuck in Lucifer's realm. Lilian is the best player at all games, even better than Aiden. If you win with Lilian, you may enter her realm. Inside her realm are the futures. Not the dreadful ones, the happy ones. No one has ever exited Lilian's realm but old myths say that you must give in on life. The next statue is Levi. Levi is the statue of proudness. In Levi's realm, you will feel proud of everything that is good. All the substandard memories of your life will be forgotten . To enter Levi's realm, you must gamble with his sister, Paris. To exit Levi's realm, you must kill a friend. Then, only you can exit. Many people have gone mad after leaving Levi's realm. The next statue is Paris. Paris is the statue of Humbleness. To enter Paris' realm, you must enter a secret statement. "Love is strong. Death is great. Ice is cold but fire is hot. Time is long and sacred to me. Just as proudness is sacred to thee. This is the statement of my great son. He knows better than you. But he is not humble a s thou.

To begin your starting journey, wings of prey and claws of predators. The star must shine on the darkest night. Might you be old or young, you are never curious enough. Although this is a long oath, it will be a long time before you come out. Answer this riddle and you may enter. What has a ring but no finger. Can you figure this out? If you can't you must leave. Before Lucifer comes. At midnight at the very last minute, my guards will come. Escape and hide in my hair and all will be safe. I will close this statement by saying, good luck." **To exit Paris' realm you must enter another sacred statement.** "Hearts of power. Diamonds of hour. THe glory is finished here. How can you leave like so easily? To Give up my power? No. I must pursue it. Here is the part you must memorize. Fish jump in lakes and clouds are in the sky. Birds are colorful but weird. Can you can you oh how. To the raw skew view fur big rot way six cat. got here for the great and gruesome dragon person cat. Couldn't Barton to get fish. **The sacred statements of Paris are indeed long. You must memorize them. one wrong pronunciation or word and you are back to Lucifer's realm. The next statue is Mary. Mary is the statue of music, sleep, and good dreams. To enter her realm you must enter a long statement. Mary is half sister to Paris** This is her statement. " To the great canyon. Past the oceans. To the shorelines of thee. Lies my sister, awaken and unseen. She dreams of war. of blood and death. But inside her is light. And in the light is love and happiness, but comes in the price of loss. And your soul you must toss. To awaken the foreseen." In Mary's realm, you get lost in sleep, dreams, and the music. It can be dangerous... but pleasing to some certain creatures. Mary guards and chases away Lucifer. Her and Rovana are the only ones who can block out Lucifer. To exit Mary's realm, you must drink from a goblet of wine without acting drunk. The next statue is Rovana. Rovana is the statue of luck and hope. To enter her realm, you must scream

John thought about the myth. He didn't realize there was a HighFli in the air until it started beeping furiously. John finally glanced up.

A bright blue HighFli slid down to Planet Death. The person inside had an oxygen bubble covering their face. John couldn't see clearly and squinted his eyes. He only knew the person inside had long and wavy hair with light caramel highlights, like John. Her HighFli had Casoli and Jokulan tattoos stuck to it. She had an emerald green light connected to her HighFli which showed that this girl was an Earth Mage, like Carla.

Suddenly, like lightning hitting John, John realized that the girl in the HighFli might actually be Carla. John had the power of super senses. John squinted at the person inside the HighFli. With the most glee and triumph he'd ever had, John sprinted toward the HighFli. It was actually Carla! After months of waiting, John finally found Carla! Hope surged through him as he ran faster and faster.

Carla looked like she hadn't slept in days, maybe even months. John wondered how worried she was.

John frantically moved around his arms, trying to cause a lot of motion. Carla didn't seem to notice him. John ran even closer to the Highfli, but he was still so, so far away. How could he get there fast enough? John could run, but he couldn't run at seventy miles per hour. John's confidence, glee, and triumph slowly disappeared and it was quickly replaced with sadness, impatience, helplessness, and sorrow. Carla was going to leave soon, John was sure of it.

John screamed as loud as he could. In fact, he screamed so loud that he could hear his own voice echoing off the sand. Although John was sure he was loud, it was impossible for Carla to hear him.

Chapter 20

John felt a heavy loss. He imagined being back at his house with his family and friends. Instead, he was stuck on this filthy land with deaths here and there. John missed Frank and Aspen. He couldn't believe Aspen had betrayed him. He thought that she was loyal. And Frank . . . poor Frank, he could never come home for dinner now.

Frank's mother was at home making dinner for her son who would never come home—making supper for a son who was in his grave.

John was on his own now. Well . . . he had Riley… John suddenly felt grateful to his passionate, loyal, and loving companion. John didn't care that Riley was a dog. Riley was *his* dog.

John reached back to pat his companion on the head. John didn't feel that shaggy and crazy hair.

"Riley?" John asked.

No response.

John slowly turned his head around, hoping that Riley was there. John closed his eyes, afraid of what he might see. His eyes slowly fluttered open. Riley was nowhere to be seen.

John felt panic rising up in his throat. What will happen to Riley? John forced himself to calm down. After a few moments of deep breathing, John pulled out his book of quotes.

"There wounds never show on the body that are deeper and more hurtful than anything bleeds."

What does that mean? John wondered. Did it mean that the loss of Frank, Aspen, and Riley was greater than any wound John has ever had?

After reading the quote, John felt a bit better. He was going to find Riley. But that dream faded away as quickly as it had come. The vast lands stretched out in all directions. Riley could be anywhere. It was getting dark too, the sun was halfway below Death already. Maybe John should just sleep and find Riley in the morning. *NO! I must find riley!* John reminded himself. John chose a random direction to go to.

John surged forward toward the sun. John still couldn't see any movement, no living beings. When had Riley even disappeared? *She stopped barking about 7 hours ago.* It didn't matter now. Within 7 hours she could be anywhere. Was it even possible for John to find Riley? Probably not. John didn't think so. So why was he still looking? After all, it was impossible. *But you might have thought it was impossible for Aspen to betray you.* A tiny voice in John's head told him. So it was probably possible for John to find Riley.

The sun had completely disappeared by now. John needed to go to sleep. He heard that when the sun went down in a remote area the *Anumi Kanwai* came out. John muttered a quick protection spell for a force shield before he fell asleep.

John had a dream that he was falling. Down below him he could hear a voice saying, "Come here… Come here…" John heard a terrible screaming erupt from his throat that sounded like a mannagal. All around him, he was surrounded by many different creatures including Xenomorph and The Pale Man. They were clawing at him. Siren Head's shadow loomed over John. John backed away and bumped into Eyeless Jack who was taller than John. The creatures were closing in on John. John could feel sweat trickling down the side of his face. Suddenly a hole opened up beneath John's feet. John could feel at least fifty eyes on him all laughing and mocking John. John didn't have time to feel embarrassed even with Jeff the Killer throwing his knife down on John.

When the knife hit John, he immediately woke up, freezing from his nightmares. Frozen sweat was covering every inch of John. John was in a burning hot desert but still, he was freezing cold.

The sun in the desert was just past the horizon, illuminating the whole sky with colors from deep red to rose gold. That would mean that today was January 1st of the year 83967. Or if he went the Casoli way, it would be 93875978958347, but John didn't want to go in detail on how the date was so long.

John knew that meant it had been 9 months since he had disappeared. Had it really been that long? He felt his side. Where was Riley?!

Chapter 21

John spotted Riley in the middle of the desert lying there in the sand. It hurt John's heart to see her like that. Riley was curled up right there in the middle of the sand with a deep cut lashed down her back. Blood was welling up and Riley's golden-white fur was soaked in blood. It looked as if Riley had been cut by a long, sharp, and thin, claw. John felt a mixed feeling between anger and sadness.

"Riley!" John yelled but Riley didn't reply.

Riley just laid there in howling pain. John wanted to help her, but she seemed about a mile away. There is absolutely no way to help her and John knew that. Even Aspen probably couldn't have solved the mystery, no matter how much John believed she could have. John cried out to Riley but Riley couldn't hear him. John cried out again, and Riley could hear John but it was too much pain for her to turn around. John already knew that. He cried out over and over again, but Riley couldn't do anything. John wanted Riley to leap into his arms with joy, instead of lying there bleeding to death.

John shouldn't have brought Riley to this trip anyway.

He shouldn't have done it, he shouldn't have done it, he shouldn't have done it.

John repeatedly cried out to Riley. Riley was helpless and couldn't do anything. The long cut that scratched down her back was soaked with blood and was bleeding out even more every second. Black red and blue colors filled Riley's back and she let out a low groan of pain. John clapped three times and for Riley to look up at him. Riley turned her head and John could see her muscles straining with her head weight. John looked into Riley's eyes and could see her once cheerful brown eyes dulling out with pain. Riley let out a little moan. John's heart fell to pieces. He couldn't just stand there!

But what *could* John do? John had no medicine, alcohol, bandages, or even a band aid. John couldn't just stand here while Riley was dying. John felt tears rolling down his face. John raised a hand to wipe the tears.

"I am so so sorry Riley." John whispered. Riley just whimpered. A sudden blue flash of light blinded John. Next to him Aspen was there. Huge, feathery, blue wings were sprouting from her shoulders. John stared at her.

"Am I that cool?" Aspen asked, wiggling her eyebrow.

Aspen immediately started cursing at John while he was crying hysterically. John only managed to catch the words simp, idiot, stupid, and killer. Aspen rambled on for a couple minutes about incoherent things.

John rubbed his eyes. "Wha-a-a-a?" John mumbled.

"You can't just leave Riley there, DYING!" Aspen yelled at John's face. Ferocity was burning inside Aspen. John could feel it.

Aspen stretched her hand back.

"Wait what are you doing?" John asked nervously.

"What am I doing? What are you doing?" Aspen yelled madly but not without a hint of panic in it.

John groaned. Aspen snarled. Aspen picked up her hand and wacked John in the face. John's face burned from the slap.

Aspen flapped her feathery wings as a halo shimmered to life above her head. Aspen wiggled her eyebrows again. John just groaned.

"Aren't I cool?" Aspen asked. John shook his head and Aspen raised her eyebrow. John was annoyed at Aspen's adamant attitude. For once, his mind was off Riley, who was lying there. *Yeah John, you left Riley dying there!*

John rushed over to Riley who was lying under a tree. It was the most sad thing Aspen had ever seen. *Oh wow John! This is how you think your thoughts? Your lame.* Yeah yeah, anyway.

Aspen went over to Riley and performed her voodoo magic, muttering along.

"Daisy curses yellow roses, medicine healing, protect this dog! Wackaboo!"

A huge flood of blood rushed from Riley's wound.

"Sorry, can't help you." Aspen muttered under her breath. She staggered a bit and walked into a mysterious blue portal that John was sure hadn't been there before.

"It's better if you let her die, John! She will be without pain," she called over her shoulder as she stepped through the mysterious portal.

John started sobbing hysterically. But John wouldn't let her die. Riley loved John and John loved Riley. After all, that was the way it was supposed to be: two friends, forever and always.

John rushed over, cut himself in the wrist and let Riley drink his blood. John knew it would be painful. Riley howled with pain, matching John's desperate cries. It was sad music to the world. It was midnight and people were crying and dogs were howling. That's the way life was after all. They sat there for a while, motionless. Riley, who could only whimper softly, began to feel less and less pain as time passed.

John felt bad. He shouldn't have led Riley to this planet. It was all his fault, and there was no one else to blame. If only he hadn't been obsessed with his stupid HighFli. John should have been with Carla, who had probably gone head over heels worried. He also missed Carson, who was probably heartbroken.

John took out his knife and pointed it at Riley. Something in his mind screamed that maybe it would be better to let Riley die a painless death.

John couldn't. He wouldn't.

John didn't care if he had to battle the beast all over again. He wanted his life back, but like his mother always said, "You cannot get everything in life."

John was sad, but not the normal kind of sad. He felt an overwhelming amount of grief. So much so that he could barely see through the curtains of despair that covered his mind. However, along with that unbearing grief came anger. Anger at all those who had died because of his stupid mistakes.

John followed big footprints leading away from the howling Riley. He pulled out the little enchanted knife that had been Frank's last gift. He promised himself that no one else would die at his expense. And today he would avenge all the lost ones.

John noticed his silver-midnight colored scales were turning white. It was a searing sort of white, and it burned through anything he touched. He couldn't tell if it burned with anger or with grief.

He continued following the tracks with memories of John's lost ones.

His mother, Violet. His father, Oliver. His sister, Crystal. Carla, who was alive and waiting for John with nothing to do.

John wasn't going to let go. This newfound rage was completely foreign to his body but he found that he depended on it. John wanted to kill those who had hurt his loved ones. He couldn't take all of the death anymore. John vowed to put an end to it, even if it meant sacrificing a couple of lives along the way.

You know what John, I don't care about your stupid thoughts. I am gonna interrupt if you don't mind. AHEM. Anyway, as I flew away I felt someone behind me. I didn't want to turn around so I clawed behind me. I didn't feel anything which was creepy. Suddenly as soon as it happened, someone put a blindfold around me. "AHHH" I screamed.

John could feel the beast's deadness weighing heavily on his shoulder. He would do it. He had to do it. He should do it and he would. John at last found the beast. It was dawn on the day he would avenge his life. John grunted and walked along the muddy, big, footprints. No one would kill Riley. John could almost feel the loving, soothing voice of his mother.

"Never give up my John!" John heard her voice tease. She tickled John in the stomach. John laughed and poked her on the chin. "Stay strong my little one!" The next day she was gone. John felt tears starting to leak out of his eyes. He continued to tromp along when John fell into the sand. John was sinking fast. John pushed the sand beside him to get himself up but there was no luck. John couldn't avenge them. His red aura began to fade.

No! I need to stay strong! John did some quick thinking and muttered, "Alseeto Cathanalo".

John began to levitate high up into the air. John twisted around and set himself down. He had traveled the world his dad couldn't survive and tramped through 3 quick sands to get to this beast. It was a green dragon, bright and green and the dragon was eating… ALIEN! John didn't want to kill the dragon. It was so pretty. And well… majestic. With beautiful green leafy wings to pearly green horns. The dragon had very shiny scales and very sharp claws in which John shivered at. John could almost feel the soul of the dragon, a girl around his age with piercing blue eyes and long white hair. She gave a friendly wave at him with a bright smile and John felt surprisingly guilty.

The girl had a long green dress that the girl waved around happily. The girl mouthed, "Need anything?"

John felt even more guilty, but his loss took over him. He would not let this dragon take more. He had to kill the dragon. John went over to the dragon as quiet as he could. He only had one strike so he made the best of it. The dragon turned its head around and its inner soul, the little girl, gasped. " Oh hi!" She giggled, "Excuse my poor manners but I am hungry and finishing my dinner, perhaps we can talk another time?" John shook his head. The girl brushed some dust off her dress. She grinned. John felt something was wrong with her.

The girl rose up high in the air and as fast as it happened, she went right through John's face, making John pass out.

John blinked open his eyes. Where was he? Was his name even John? John felt that his name was actually Jessica so why was he calling himself John? Was he even a male? Jessica looked up to see herself facing the weird dragon girl. By force, Jessica bowed down to the dragon girl. John couldn't move. Was his name John? Questions filled John's head and curiosity filled John's eyes. The dragon girl patted John on the head.

"There, Jessica!" She exclaimed with excitement beaming through her voice.

And then he found it. The source of all salvation, all John's hope, was in front of him. John rubbed at his eyes.

Could it be? No, it can't be. Carla's shiny Highfli was rearing around the corners of his vision.

Had she really come back for him?

This time around, he made sure to wave all of his body parts, screaming and shouting as he jumped up and down. The dragon girl looked towards John with mild confusion, realizing that the head she had been petting seconds ago turned out to be quite the opposite of a dragon.

"Carla! Carla! It's me , John!" shouted John on the top of his lungs. Carla must have caught sight of John's tiny figure as the Highfli began to make a slow descent towards John.

Flopping down onto the ground from exhaustion, John closed his eyes with relief.

Carla was here.

Carla had found him.

All was good.

Chapter 22

John flew past stars on the ride with the Highfli. He started calculating how fast they were going which was impossible while Aspen was munching on Jokulasatees.

"Can you be quiet for once?" John begged. Aspen silenced him with a ferocious glare.

"Can't your dog be quiet either? If she can be loud I can be loud and I'm not that loud."

"Yeah, but Riley's a dog! Your breed is supposed to be nice, kind, and quiet!"

Aspen fumed around and then decided to be too nice, kind, and quiet.

"Oh, be quiet." Carson suddenly put in. John realized that this was probably the best choice. Aspen took out her favorite knives and started swinging them around. One poked John in the back.

Carla had collapsed from exhaustion the moment John had entered her Highfli. John had taken over and flew back to the base on Jokula, though he didn't have enough gas to make it to his home.

The entire ride back had been completely silent, with Carla knocked out and unaware that she had just saved her boyfriend and with John closely following the directions, ensuring that he would make it back safe. They half-crash landed into the base, and John was immediately taken away to emergency centers, where medics had determined that John's many wounds would need to be treated. This meant that John could not truly return home until all of his wounds were set and he recovered. It had been weeks in the hospital area, and no visitors had been allowed.

But today was the day. Today, Carson would be picking John up from the hospital. Carson had volunteered to send John home, where Carla was supposedly waiting. Carla was still unaware that she had managed to save John, believing that the auto-pilot setting on the Highfli had taken her home. Of course, in reality, it had been John driving the Highfli back.

The two still had not been able to talk, and much less be able to have an actual conversation.

"Jeez, just because I have tougher Jokula skin doesn't mean you can poke me, it still hurts.

"Just because Riley's a dog doesn't mean she can't shut up so SHUT UP, RILEY."

John was seriously annoyed because Riley had been eating a lot and getting pretty fat. She'd pawed John for Fupinwites 13 times now in the past three hours. Fupinwites were Riley's favorite dog treats. She adored them. This one time, Riley ate all the fupinwites and then threw up because she had eaten too much. Riley needed to shut up.

But John couldn't bring himself to shut her up. The past year on Dead was pretty nice with Riley, mainly because of her helpful barks and now it didn't seem fair to shut her up. John nudged Riley playfully and gave her a belly rub. Riley simply barked at John with all teeth. John sighed. Riley was acting very weird these days. Carson suddenly lit up.

"And we are home!"

It felt so good to hear the word home again. Home is where he would be. Home is where he lived. Home is… well John knew it meant everything to him. John gave Carson a grateful smile. Carson nodded his head.

"It is where you should be."

"Thanks." John simply said. He didn't really have anything to say.

Home started racing toward them. John almost wanted to jump off and run to the house he had built for himself.

John shook himself, no. He would die if he jumped off a moving Highfli and Carla needed him.

Finally, after what seemed like a long time, Carson landed. John thought, what would he say to Carla? After all those minutes passing. John slowly opened the door.

"Carla is in bad shape." Carson warned.

"I can handle that."

John pushed the door open. Everything seemed to come back to him. The lovely smell of Carla's freshly baked cookies, the smell of horse poop and the whiniest of horses and best of all, Carla. Riley jumped out the door and ran over to Carla despite being fat and slow. Carla just stared in amazement.

"Wha-wha-what? How?" Carla slowly said.

"Miss me?" John asked.

"John, of course I missed you!"

Carla ran straight over and whispered,

"You missed college."

"I missed you." John replied. He was so happy he couldn't breathe. Suddenly Riley started hacking out barf all over the lawn. Carla quickly ushered Riley inside and gave John a weak smile.

"She is pregnant, John. Riley, I mean."

That sentence seemed like everything. Almost. It explained why Riley had been so fat and slow and why she ate so much. It was for her babies. John quickly went inside and grabbed a bowl from the top cabinet.

John suddenly realized just how long he had been missing. Carla must have been so sad. John felt guilty. If only he hadn't been so obsessed with that stupid HighFli.

John missed the outside world, feeling what it was like to feel the lush green grass. He missed the ladybug that had landed on his eyebrow when John was 7. John missed the butterflies that danced around his head whenever he sneezed.

And most of all John missed Carla. John used his finger to draw a quick sketch in the air of Carla.

Carson and Aspen walked in, watching John and Carla gush over Riley.

Carla pointed to a pan of freshly baked cookies that were cooling on the oven, which John proceeded to gulf down.

"So," began Carla. "How was your adventure?"

John, whose face was still stuffed with cookies, was unable to respond.

The group laughed a little at the sudden silence, and John turned around to admire the world around him, breathing in the fresh air that was laced with the scent of something sweet.

The scent of home.

Epilogue

"Hi, is the camera working?" I fumbled with the controls.

"Of course it is, you glowing blue head!" Carla, my sister, teased playfully.

"Take that back you knucklehead!" I shot back.

John buried his face into Riley's fur and moaned, "What am I gonna do?"

"Shut up." I yelled.

Carson amicably slapped me on the back. "Good one!" He gave me a cheerful grin.

"Are you grinning at me!?" I summoned a ball of hot, blue, powerful, flames.

"Whoa! Don't break the camera Asp!" Carson laughed.

Oh right. I was on camera.

"Whoops!" I easily said. I promptly apologized as I purposely stomped on Carson's foot.

"Asp! Cut it OUT!" Carson yelled. "Sorry! No can do!" I joked.

Carson glanced at his watch.

"It's time for me to go back to my house man!" Carson told John. "Awww! Too bad."

"Too good!" I declared cheerfully. "Aspen!" Carson groaned as he started floating up in the air. And then shot into the air with a loud whoop. I blushed. Just a little.

It was 30 years since John had taken me back to earth. You want to know how I even got to Death? I was 7 human years old. Me and my older sister, Carla were playing. Carla had introduced her new friend Emma. Emma was very pretty. She had long beautiful blond hair and was very tall. She was a furry and had very pretty albino ears. (Albino was a kind of Wolf.) Right away I knew something was wrong with Emma. Not physically, not mentally, but she was filled with hatred towards me. I knew that when I first asked her if she wanted some gator. She had asked for a private chat and Carla had agreed as if she made MY decisions. Emma had come up to me and sadly, annoyingly, bossily, she said, "Look! Your sister is pretty. You aren't. Stay away from me you disgusting *Cara Fea*!" I had burst into tears. I had run home and my mom had yelled at me for breaking a glass vase. No doubt about Emma being the nasty devil. I even wrote a diary about those days.

Dear diary,

Emma yelled at me today for swinging with Carla. Is that bad? I don't think I did anything wrong. . . I think Emma just wants Carla to herself. I'm having nightmares about Emma. She always ends up yelling about how much of a freak I am. I don't like it. Mom and Carla don't believe me. Carla is very mad at me. It's all Emma's fault.

Dear diary,

Mom says i'm grounded for a week and i can't do any magic. That's not fair! Magic is my life! Emma says i'm a piece of bull poop. I don't know what that means... Emma is mean. Carla says i'm being a pathological liar. My arms really hurt.

Dear diary,

I saw a black shadow today. It creeps me. I don't like it. I have goosebumps. It's been following me the whole day. Make it stop! Make it go away!

At that point in my life, I got kidnapped. Ba boom! Yeah! Fun! Very fun. Uh huh! No. It wasn't fun at all. It was EXTREMELY boring. I was so bored. Anyway moving on. Carson left. Blah blah blah. I sighed and pulled out my magic staff.

"Wha- Whoa!" John said, "Where did you get that?".

"No where." I sneered. John pouted.

"Oh come on!".

"Let's create a meme."

Carla hurried down a hallway. Ten boring minutes later, she came out with a camera. Carla started the camera.

"Dude! You're just so ugly!" I told Carla.

"Honey, do I look like a mirror?" Carla replied.

"You just got microwaved and a bit toasted inside!" John yelled cooly. Carla stopped filming and we all laughed.

I muttered some curse and my wings popped out and one of the wings hit John in the head. I giggled. John gave me a loopy frown. I grinned.

"Now let's go to sleep." Carla said quickly. She pushed John into their room as I curled up on the couch.

I thought about today. It has been 5 years since John brought me back from Dead. 5 years. No extra days. So if it was 5 years… then I would be 15. At midnight. And right now it is 11:23 p.m. I waited. But as you know I easily get bored so I fell asleep at 11:25 p.m. I woke up to heavy footsteps. It was 11:58. I shivered as I remembered the time I got kidnapped 12 years ago. I felt goose bumps creeping up my arm. I pulled up my blanket even more as I curled up on the couch. The only funny thing was I was glowing like a beacon. I tried to laugh but my voice wouldn't work.

11:59. The time flashed in my head as I used my magic. Was that something dragging outside. I curled up even tighter.

Five more seconds… 4...3...2...1… BAM!

Someone opened the door as the lights flickered on. Balloons crowded my vision and I managed to see that said, "Happy Birthday!" I groaned and rubbed my eyes. I pushed myself out of my bed to see Carson standing there with a big grin.

"Happy Birthday! I hope that you celebrate the day you came back from Dead."

We are all a little broken,

But last time I checked,

Broken crayons still

Color the same. *-Trent Shelton*

Don't cry when the sun is gone,

The tears won't let you see the stars.

Courage is the power

To let go of familiar

You are not broken

You are breaking through

The most difficult phase of life

Is not when no one understands you

It's when you cannot understand yourself

Never give up hope

For hope hasn't yet given up on you

You just let go of yourself every time

Push yourself because

no one else is going to do it for you.

If people are doubting how far you can go

Go so far that you cannot hear them anymore

Happiness is not by chance but by choice.

Acknowledgements

I would like to thank Claire Qu for making this book possible, Madeleine Ye and Derek Qu for being good editors, and Janelle Lee for being a good partner to work with. My parents for encouraging me, and to my dog for keeping me happy. My amazing computer, which stayed with me and didn't lag. My bed, for offering rest periods in between writing, and of course I would like to thank all of my friends for being my friends. I would like to thank My chair and electricity for helping me. I would like to thank my tired fingers for typing a lot.

- Chris Wu

I acknowledge Madeleine Ye and Derek Qu for being helpful editors. Without them, I would not have gotten this far into writing the book. I thank my chickens for squawking every morning at 6:30 A.M and kicking dust around the yard and amusing me. I appreciate the work and dedication that Chris Wu put in to write this book. I would like to thank Claire Qu for making this all possible. I would also like to thank my parents for encouraging me. I thank Ella Yi, Mia Zheng, Lindsay Zhang, and Madeleine Ye for being great friends despite my recklessness. I would like to thank my brain for coming up with things to write down words in this book. I thank my hands for typing half of this book. I also thank my chair so that I could sit somewhere while writing in this book. I also thank electricity because without it, I wouldn't be able to write in this book. I thank my brother for being the best brother I could ever have.

- Janelle Lee